For my wife Heather
For standing by me through this long process

RANDOM LIVES

Second Edition

RANDOM LIVES

Michael Haueisen II

Published by Tate Publishing & Enterprises, LLC
127 E. Trade Center Terrace | Mustang, Oklahoma 73064 USA
1.888.361.9473 | www.tatepublishing.com

Tate Publishing is committed to excellence in the publishing industry. The company reflects the philosophy established by the founders, based on Psalm 68:11,
"The Lord gave the word and great was the company of those who published it."

Published in the United States of America

ISBN: 978-1-68270-385-4
1. Fiction / Crime
2. Fiction / Mystery & Detective / General
15.09.24

Table of content

Chapter 1

It was another lousy early spring night. He could feel the chill that remained. He still needed a heavy long sleeve shirt at night. He wore a pair of old worn out blue jeans, a dark blue knit hat and black steel-toe work boots. Only a few cars seemed to pass by. They ranged from the standard sedan to the now ever present sports utility vehicle. He casually walked down the sidewalk, passing the houses in the neighborhood. The sidewalk was old and cracked. Bits of grass and weeds broke through as time went by aging the cement. The houses covered in shadows and dim slices of light making them all an ugly shade of orange from the street lights and silhouetted in shadows. At that time of night, only a handful of the house's had lights in the window. He hated the fact that even though it was spring, night time still came early. The only joy he got out of it was that it let him hide in the shadows of the night sky. The weather hadn't been that nice. Only the day before it had been in the 60's and that day it was down to the low 40's dropping to the mid or low 30's by night. A slight wind started to pick up.

He couldn't help but to shiver, thinking of how he never liked the cold. He zipped up his dark grey fleece shirt the rest of the way. As the collar lifted up, he felt his neck. His fingers passed over the scars on his neck. The memories started to flood back.

It was college, his sophomore year. The time was near the end of the semester and he was ready to get his practice exam back. The class was a medium size room with faded white walls and dirty, trampled forest green carpet. The desks were small and cramped and never were comfortable to him with his huskiness. His math professor handed him back the practice exam. It had a mark on it that he had not expected, an "F" written in bright red ink. His teacher leaned a little closer to him and said loud enough so that the whole class could hear, "Maybe you should try for an easier career in the end, try a custodian or flipping burgers or scrubbing toilets." The whole class erupted in laughter. It was the most embarrassing moment of his life. Feeling as if everything he had been working for was worthless, he got up out of his desk and ran to the door almost running into the wall in the process. He tore open the door and flew down the hall ready to cry his eyes out.

Later that night, he decided to talk to his teacher about his grade and about what she said in class. He knew he wasn't the worlds smartest but he didn't deserve what was said. He could only think about how the class acted, it was no longer the thought of how hard he had studied and worked on the exam. He walked down the sparsely lit hall. Pictures of old professors and deans that once worked at the college looked down on him. His eyes took in the ugly yellow paint job that took up the ceiling and the top half of the walls, and followed it down to the bottom half that had oak paneling that met up with a grey fake marble floor. With the old lights hanging down, he had crazy thoughts of horror movies. How the lights and the hallway looked, he could recall scenes from horror movies and wondered how many of them were actually based off of true stories. As he walked, he brushed the thought away as his nerves began to rise.

Seeing her door, he drew in a sharp

breath to steady his nerves but it only slowed them, fore with each step closer, he wanted to shake and run away but he needed to do this. He got to her door; it looked to be oak like the paneling with the glass having that bubble-like distortion and he could see some light coming from inside. He knocked on the door but there was no answer. "Mam, are you here?" he said in a slightly cracking voice. He knocked again but harder, the door opened a little bit. She didn't pull the door all the way shut he thought. He opened the door a bit more and peered inside. No one was there.

He walked in the office slowly like an animal wandering into a trap. He thought he might as well wait for her for at least a few minutes in case she did come back. The light came from a small desk lamp. It was just enough to see around the room with its few items and features. Just like out in the hall, there was that same ugly yellow paint job and the oak paneling. The smell of the office over powered his nose, long old cigarettes and the burning ashes filled the air. He could see another door on the right wall that he thought was a closet.

Her desk maybe mahogany was set on an angle near the back wall. It had some papers laying on it, probably homework or practice exams from other classes. There was a small dark grey or light black (he couldn't figure out which color in the bad lighting) ash tray sat on the left side of the desk filled with old smashed cigarettes. He felt that either she was a chain smoker or just plain too lazy to empty the thing. On the left wall was a bookshelf that was cluttered with books and folders along with a mantel clock that read 10:57 p.m. Behind the desk was a picture that he couldn't make out what it was from the glare of the light from the desk lamp. He walked up to the picture; he was curious what it was. He felt that as he approached the picture, his hip bumped the chair a little making a light creaking noise as it turned. He looked at it closely; it was a picture of his teacher with an old governor outside the library at the college. It had to be from long time ago because he just couldn't believe that she was once that thin.

"What the heck are you doing in my office?" he could hear her say from behind him in her gruff but shrill voice. He turned around and she was standing in the doorway. The only thought that passed through his head was that maybe it was the door he heard and not the chair. She was a larger woman that had a nasty sneer on her face almost all the time. Her old brown eyes glared at him and he felt that it also went into his soul, burning it from him. Her red lipstick looked cracked and well beyond the age of being applied that morning. He could see her yellow stained teeth through her sneer and how perfect they were. Too perfect he thought, had to be dentures. She was wearing a red button-up shirt and a floral print skirt and scuffed up black heels. Her graying hair was still up in a bun. She repeated herself, "What the HECK are you doing in my office?!" Her voice was only getting higher and more enraged as the sentence came out. She walked in the office a few steps and closed the door behind her with a slam. She walked towards him.

"I need to talk to you about what you said in class..." he started to say. She walked up to him, grabbed his shoulder and gave it a small rough shake. Her grip was vice like and sent pain shooting into his shoulder and arm as her thumb nail dug in more and more. She said, "I don't owe you any explanation about what I say." She let his shoulder go with a final quick shake and backed up as few feet and began pointing to the door to tell him to leave. He felt the world fade away. The dark pulse started.

He lunged at her, with his arms and fingers stretched out. He closed the short distance between them quickly. His fingers wrapped around her large neck as best as they could. She slammed back into the wall with all of his weight rushing at her. She had a stunned look on her face but it quickly changed to anger and fear. Out of desperation to live, she clawed his hands and arms hoping to get him to release his grip. She gasped trying to draw air as she tried to yell for help that she knew would not come. He then felt her hands grab his neck and tighten their grip; a final desperate act to save her life. As she struggled, his hands twisted on her neck and began turning her aging white skin into roughly rubbed red. The more his grip tightened, she could feel her air supply quickly going away. As she fought him, her high-heels slipped on the floor making her fall to the floor pressed against the wall. He followed with a natural motion to the ground leaving him in a crouched position. He pushed with more of his weight to keep her from getting her feet under her. Her voice cracked in and out from the pressure he continued to put upon her throat. His left knee pressed into her stomach to heighten the pain and to help make it harder for her to breath. Her long fingernails dug into his skin as her feet kicked wildly. The feeling of burning and being cool at the same time raced through his neck. He tightened his grip even more. Her screams cut into gasps and choking. He saw as her eyes started to roll up into her head. The moments seemed to take forever; soon after; she no longer drew breath. Her eyes seemed to almost immediately glaze over as the life left her body leaving the eyelids ever so slightly open. Her body lay still with her arms fallen at her side. Her feet were spread out with one heel still on her left foot but her right one was just holding onto her big toe. The jaw of her mouth seemed to just hang open showing a slight sign of saliva coming out of the corners.

He let go of her neck and slid back a little falling on his rear and could feel himself shaking. He sat there watching her body waiting for her to make a move of any kind. He could feel himself willing her to make a movement of any kind to show that she still lived. The feelings in him said that she was dead and he did it. Turning back or apologizing were far out the question. He lifted up his hands to look at his palms. He wanted to scream, cry and kick anything he could. The feelings overwhelmed him for a moment but were quickly pushed back. He turned his head to see the clock; it read 11:05 p.m. It felt like hours had past instead of just mere minutes. He looked down at his shirt and saw there was blood on it. As he looked, he saw that his hands and forearms where scratched up and bleeding slightly. He reached up and felt his neck. Through the blood, he could feel open points with blood slowly coming out. He could not tell how many of them there where but he knew it would be hard to hide them. He pulled his handkerchief out of his pocket and wrapped it around his neck to hide the wounds. With the cool weather outside, he could wear turtleneck sweaters to hide the wounds but would have to come up with a way to explain them to those that saw them. That would be something to think about another time. Quickly he pulled off his sweat shirt that he had wrapped around his waist. He pulled it on to hide the blood on his body. He stood up and went to open the door. It would only open a small portion; the bulk of her body was in the way. He started to yank at the door repeatedly. With each yank, he could hear the door creak and crack. After a minute or two of it, the door finally opened up just enough for him to squeeze through.

With luck, the police in the town were lazy and the investigation into his teacher's death went nowhere. The police had said that she had many issues with staff members and many old boyfriends. His luck let the police look at her boyfriends and never take a look at the students at his school. They told the reporters that many of her old boyfriends where abusive and a few had even tried killing her. This included her current boyfriend that just got out of jail the day before for assault. The case went cold and was never talked about again within a few months of the investigation stalling.

He could no longer remember if that was the first time he killed or the first time that he listened to the pulse. He no longer shook at the memory or whenever he delivered death. The time had changed so much of the world he grew up in but some parts never changed. Death would never change for him. It would always bring him delight and peace. Once the pulse started, it wouldn't subside till death had made an appearance. He didn't care who they were or what they did. The pulse picked them and they all had to die. He had listened to it for so long. He didn't want to think of what his life would be if it went away. He felt that his life would be hollow and lonely without it. It was as close to a best friend has he could ever have.

The pulse had kicked back again. It turned him to the house to his left. He turned down a cracking driveway. The house was two stories with an attached garage. A white paint job covered the walls, dark blue trim and a few bushes by the front door with lights on in a hand full of windows. He walked calmly around the back of the garage. He knew there had to be a door to get in. He found it quickly. It was unlocked.

In the dim light coming through the windows of the garage door from the streetlights, he could see a small sedan. The door to the house was up a small set of stairs near the front of the garage. He made his way past the clutter that took up what little space the car left in the garage. Items like buckets and old plant pots lined the wall. He tripped on a random cinder block lying on the ground. He cursed the block and whoever left the damned thing in his way. He used the car balance as he went. He quietly stepped up the stairs and stood next to the door. He could hear someone inside. It sounded like the kitchen was on the other side of the door. All he could hear was the clatter of ceramic dishes clanking together. He grabbed the door knob, the pulse grew stronger. There was no longer a chance to turn back. He threw the door open and went in the room with all his rage and pulsing desire.

Chapter 2

The days were still decent enough; some days you could even get away with a short sleeve shirt during the day. Revan decided to ride his black 04' Honda CBR1000RR to work. As he road, he felt younger than his late 20's. His 6 foot frame laid atop the bike as he maneuvered through traffic. His silver necklace with a silver dragon pendent hung against the inside of his leather jacket. His hate for suits led him to wear what he considered to be normal cloths. He wore a grey and black hooded sweatshirt under his leather jacket and blue cargo jeans with his steel toe boots. The weather in spring was goofy with it being warm yet cool at the same time, you could walk around in a short sleeve for the time being but riding needed a long sleeve.

The office was built out past the airport near the mall on east Sternberg Road for quick access to the high way. He chose to have it based in Muskegon because it was his hometown, many years ago. The ride from his house was a nice slow drive. He cursed a few drivers in his helmet for not watching out. He decided to ride down the expressway from his home in North Muskegon south on 120 to 31 that changed to seaway drive. He turned up hill onto Grand Haven Rd. so he could take it slow on his way to work. The silver dragon ring on the middle finger of his right hand shined in the sun as he controlled the throttle. The work the airport had done sense he had left was weird to him; they had bought up some of the property that once lined the original airport grounds and expanded the area out making the once strait shot of the road take a long windy curve so they could have a longer runway. Revan didn't care much, he didn't have to live by the airport and it helped lengthen his slow ride to the office.

He pulled into the parking lot and could see that at least everybody on his team had shown up to work on time, at least from what he could remember from their vehicles. There was something strange though; a plain black sedan that didn't sit well with him. He knew what it belonged to and he didn't want it at all. It was an FBI issue Ford Crown Victoria for one of their agents. He took off his helmet and felt the silver hoop earring in his left ear tug slightly against the inside. He walked inside carrying his scuffed up black helmet; he exchanged it for a black baseball hat with a small white dragon symbol, backwards as he always preferred it. He walked into the building looking around finally having the chance seeing it painted and put together.

The walls and ceiling were painted an eggshell white. The floor was a simple tile job that was mostly white, grey, and black spots with a few dark green spots thrown in here and there. The smell felt strange though; even though the building was new, it already was starting to smell a little bit old with dust, mildew, smoke and slight hint of stale coffee. He looked down the long hallway with doors in random places. At the end of the hall was a doorway smack in the middle as the hallway that split into opposite directions to more offices. Some offices were for research and a few set up for interrogation. The feeling that the research offices would come in the most use came over him as he looked at the wooden doors with their windows. The wing of the hallway that split to the left was all set up for light forensics lab work. The other wing was set up as minor office spaces for other police officers in the unit and a few were set aside for guest officers that could be visiting the unit or helping out.

He strolled past an office that had its door open that was full of people he recognized and one person he didn't. All but the new guy where talking amongst themselves and as he past, everybody stopped talking and looked up at him. He continued walking down to the chief's office never breaking his stride.

The feds felt they needed a chief to keep the unit in line. He couldn't give half a flip what the feds wanted; he had a job to do and wasn't going to let some suits stop him or even slow him down. He had known that police very rarely liked feds nosing into investigations and he himself hated dealing with them even when he worked for them. He knew the feds were going to try other tricks to keep an eye on every move they would make. It would be an issue that they would have to deal with when it arose. He came upon the office doorway at the end of the hallway.

The walls were painted the same eggshell white color as the hall and the floor is carpeted in a dark green. He rolled his eyes looking at the colors. Inside was a small room that had an old desk with a few papers on it and a new computer; the desk was placed in front of the doorway. A simple teal-green office chair sat behind the desk that looked as if it was stolen from an old school before it fell down. Also in the small office was a plain leather couch that looked dulled from years of use and no conditioning. It was situated to the right of the doorway for those who needed to wait for the chief. Against the far wall was a wooden door with a smoked glass window that had black lettering that say "Chief Waterfurd". He walked past the empty secretary's old oak desk; he plopped his helmet down on the desk as he went by.

He knocked on the door to the chief's office and promptly let himself in before she could say anything, and sat down in a small leather covered chair in front of her desk. Her office was lightly decorated with a few certificates and awards and the same eggshell paint job and dark green carpet. The room seemed to be collecting a smell of agitation and sweat. Her simple oak desk was new along with her comfy leather office chair. Two bookshelves stood guard behind her desk and were full of books that were heavily worn and no longer had titles that seemed legible. Her desk was sloon with papers and folders and a computer monitor shoved off to the far corner. A simple black phone was the only other item on the desk. She was sitting in her chair with the phone pressed to her ear.

She was in her mid 40's with black hair. She stood about 6'3" if you took away the low-heels. She was dressed in a red suit that said she was all business. Her average weight filled in the suit fully. Revan could tell that it was more than just weight in her suit, it was muscle and near motherly anger. To him she always looked like she could have been a librarian if she didn't like yelling at people so much or maybe that's what made her seem like a librarian. She had tired looking black eyes that looked at her desk. She wore little to almost no makeup on her face leaving her tanned white skin look pale and aged. As she held onto the phone with her right hand she tapped the desk lightly with her wedding ring. Reven felt sorry for her husband but decided that he knew what she was like long ago or was at least is just as tough as her. As she talked, Revan could see the sweat building lightly on her brow. She talked with authority and a slight hint of apology in her voice. She finally put down the phone to address him.

"Well, well, well," she said, "if it isn't Lieutenant Revan Lygar, the now constant pain in my rear. I still haven't forgotten how you work and deal with authority from last time." She was the temporary chief for the group in their first case a few years before hand. "You realize that next time you could be a little less rude and wait for me to answer the door before you barge into my office. Next time I just might shoot you." She pointed a finger at him as she talked.

He said, "I figured you would be on the phone talking as usual so I decided to let myself in. I remember that from the last few times I had seen you; you spent half the time on the phone. Any ways, you know you love working with me. I get the job done even if I have to shoot somebody to do it. So who was that? The governor trying to figure out if this is going to be a waste of time or something they can use in the next election. Or was it our friends at the gov' ready to try to pry in and make this their own thing?"

"Don't get cocky; this whole thing was your idea, no one else's. You picked the team and set most of this thing up. And yes it was the governor, they wanted to know who's butt they will get to kick if thing doesn't work out." she said pointing a pen at him making jabbing motions. "I told em' it was your butt that's on the line. They said you better not screw this up for them or this state."

"Well tell em' for me, I'll do my job and that they can kiss my foot. And if this does get screwed up, I'll kick my own but over it," he said with a shrug. "By the way, my old bosses didn't have to listen to me when I brought up the idea. They were the ones that wanted to get rid of me. They could have just let me retire or quit and be done with me but they decided to take my idea and run with it. Now let's go and do our meet and greet with the team, shall we?" He gestured toward the door. "By the way, have the holly's started jumping down our thoughts or am I going to get ambushed?" He called the reporters from both the news and the papers holly's because they tried to make every story they get into a Hollywood movie.

She told him, "I've had a few calls and request for interviews about what we're doing, who's in the group, and how much "tax" payer money is going to be blown on this." She gestured to a small stack of papers with names and numbers with hastily written nasty nick names like "Whine boy" and "Turd fisher". "You or someone around here is gonna have to talk to them sometime," she said solemnly.

"Well, it's nice to know that I'm not the only one that hates the hollys," he said with a bit of a grin. "You can have the talk. I hate those people and would rather be duct taped to the wing of a 747 than deal with them."

Chapter 3

They both got up and walked back down the hall to the office with the open door. She stood in the door way knocking on the door to get everyone's attention. "Excuse me. I'm Miss Waterfurd. I am your chief from this moment on. You were all pulled together to form a task force that specializes in tracking down serial killers in the state of Michigan and apprehending them." She said, "For some of you this is not your first time together and for the rest, welcome. We handle things here much like any police force across the country so no breaking any rules or laws. Good luck and go get 'em."

The office was actually the outer area of Revan's office. He chose a large room for the purpose. It had the same paint job and carpet as the chief's office. The outer area had a wooden conference table and chairs for the unit to sit down and talk to the right of the door. His secretary's desk sat near the wall opposite from the door. To the left of the door was a wall with another door. That door led into Revan's own office. He wanted to have a space near his office to sit down and talk with his unit.

She turned and walked back down to her office and Revan stepped in the room rolling his eyes about her last sentence. The thought that crossed his mind was that he must have stepped into some made for TV cop movie with that last line. He recognized everybody but one person. The new guy sat in a chair by the far wall. He wore a suit and sat up strait. There was only one type of person that he knew would be like that around there. He was a fed, the same style you always see. His suit neatly pressed and his desire to look as professional as possible. "Are you a fed?" Revan inquired.

"Yes I am. I'm Agent John Beareck of the FBI; I was sent here as an observer and liaison to the FBI" he said. He looked to be in his mid to late 20's, he had dark brown hair was the same as his eyes, they at least told Revan that he was full of crap just like any fed he had ever dealt with. His face seemed plain but polite hiding nervousness in his trim build. He looked as if he should have been an elementary teacher rather than an FBI agent, but Revan was sure he has a nice long story behind it. John got up to shake Revan's hand. He stood just slightly taller than Revan making him have to look lightly down into his eyes. Revan walked away shrugging him off. He never had liked feds nor did he plan to ever like them; their too uptight and inflexible with people. They think the only thing in the world is the book. Well sometimes, you have to stop reading the book and follow your instincts is how Revan's outlook was on life.

He walked up to the rest of the group and shook their hands and gave a few hugs. There was Mary Darnoise from sex crimes, Eric Bromish from homicide, Ray Dumose of auto theft, Barry Harmic of robbery, Amy Straima of organized crime, and Derek Tomas of fraud. Revan chose the group by their job and their reputation doing their job. The team had been pulled together from all over Michigan. All but one was forced to move to be part of the team but they were more than willing to do so. They also had a secretary named Melissa Scotts that would help handle messages and many other odd jobs around the office.

"Looks like we get to do this again," Barry said. "So you got us together, now what do we get to do?" His muscular 7 foot frame made his dressy leather jacket creek and stretch. The light in the room shined off of his bald head as he moved. Revan felt his piercing black eyes look over the horizontal scar on his left cheek and the vertical one through his right eye. Revan was use to the reactions and stares that he got from them and the third one on his chest. Barry returned to his spot leaning against the wall.

"Here's your first case Revan," said Melissa. Revan saw that she was wearing light blue jeans, white tennis shoes, and a white and light blue sweater. She was seated behind her desk. A desk sized calendar laid in the center. A flat screen computer monitor sat to the right of the calendar at an angle. Her hand touched Revan's when he reached for the files.

She let him take the two folders. "The first is Brian James, 32 and his girl friend Tonya Lamon, 28. They were killed a week and a half ago. They were murdered in his home in Custer on South Main Street. He was stabbed with a screw driver 17 times and she was strangled with a pillowcase. The second is Ronda Bells, 34. She was killed two days ago. She was killed in her Eastmont home on Cutter parkway southeast. She was beaten to death with a statue. There was plenty of evidence left behind by the killer at both places. They left finger prints, blood, shoe prints, and hair," she explained,

"Ok. They were all killed different ways. How are we so sure that it is the same killer?" Revan asked everyone. "Anyone have an answer? And what is the connection?"

"Well from the interviews that the locals at each scene conducted, it looks like neither the first vics or the second vic had any connection to each other," Ray spoke up.

He moved forward in the group using his athletic body to maneuver. His dark grey dress shirt, light skin, and thin mustache made Revan think of Wesley Snipes in Drop Zone. "The vics were killed in different ways, this is true, but it's the fingerprints that link them. When the locals uploaded the evidence data into the computers and it spit out the link, it got handed over to us as per the new procedure. The scene techs said that they would get back to us as soon as possible about the rest of the evidence. However, they said that so far it looks like there is only one perp involved. So what do we do next fearless leader?"

The team stood closely around Revan in a circle to listen in. Revan started, "Well let's go to each scene and get a good look around. I want us ourselves to know the area and take it in. Just looking at photos and video can't give you the feel of the scene like seeing it for yourself. I know the scene won't feel the same as when it was fresh but we have to work with what we got. So go and check them out and talk to people that knew the vics. We'll split into two groups of four. Ray, Mary, John, and myself will be one group. The other group will be Eric, Barry, Amy, and Derek. It'll take about an hour to get to Custer and about 50 minutes to an hour to get to Eastmont. My group will go to Custer and you guys go to Eastmont. Call me if you come across anything interesting. Here take the file to see what evidence is already found."

Revan handed the file for Ronda Bells to Eric. "Make sure you all look at it and know the file front to back. I don’t want anything missed that could help us. Make sure you also look at the photos in the file and take a really close look at each area they were taken,” Revan said. He turned and pointed to Barry, “You’re really good at looking for things most people miss, take a good look around especially any area not photographed. Get a hold of the techs if anything is found. When you’re done there, come back here, we'll come back also and talk about what is found. So let’s mount up.” He started to turn to leave and then stopped and looked back to say, “By the way Melissa, if anything comes up, let me know a.s.a.p., ok? And call the state police and see if they have anything they can add." She nodded her head and started through a file cabinet on the wall opposite of her desk.

John quickly stepped up to Revan as they started to leave the room. "Why do you want me to go with you? I was told that you don't like federal agents. I thought that you would try to stick me with some mindless task. My superiors had told me that I was to expect not to have a lot to do with you as the lead.

Your hate for federal agents is well known to them."

He replied, "Because I want to keep an eye on you and I have a mindless task for you tomorrow. Tomorrow I need you to get the fingerprints and DNA run through the FBI's CODIS system. If this lunatic left this much evidence behind, then he could have done something somewhere else, and I want to know about it. So let's go and don't ask stupid questions. And make sure that IAFIS was run too."

They headed out the office. Revan wasn't happy being among the last to leave at the time because a fed had to ask a stupid question. John could tell that his question had upset Revan by observing how his walking had become hurried and heavy. John followed Revan quietly making sure not to bump into him and risk angering him more as they walked out of the building.

Chapter 4

Revan was flipping through the James-Lamon folders in the front passenger seat as they drove north on US-31 to US-10 and headed East to South Main Street in Custer. The ride took them through what seemed to be endless amount of farms and forest. They could see small towns off exits of the freeway. They rode in Ray's red 98' Jeep Cherokee. "Hey Revan, can I ask you a question?" Ray inquired. "When we were all together the last time, we all sat around telling our stories but you didn't. So can I ask you, what the heck is your middle name?" Revan looked up at him with a raised eyebrow. "Well I know you like to keep to yourself. You know a lot about the rest of us from those times but we know next to nothing outside of your age and that you hate bosses. So I would just like to know this one little thing about you."

"It's Monolith, my full name is Revan Monolith Lygar," he said. It was Ray's turn to have a questioned look on his face along with the others in the Jeep. "In case you're wondering if it could possibly be my real name; no it's not. It's my name but not the name I was born with. I changed it years ago; I thought that if I changed my name then it would make it hurt less. It didn't help." Revan went back to reading the files and they all rode in silence. The questions rolled through all of their heads to ask what had happened but resigned to the fact that Revan would not tell that part of his life. As they turned onto 10 from 31, they could have turned west to Ludington but continued their trip. On 10 they passed even more farms and forest in between small Amber through bigger Scottville right into the small town of Custer.

Ray said as he pulled into the driveway, "Yo man, we're here," as he put the Jeep in park and turned it off. They all got out and started walking toward the house. The house was a one story with a car-port off to the right side of the house. A green 1986 Ford F150 sat under the carport rusting with the weather until a new owner would come to take it home. A fading grey paint job looked to be peeling from many years of not being scraped and repainted. A front door and side door seemed to be the only ways in and out of the house. A modest front yard was spread in the front with a slightly larger yard in the back. The grass was still trying to regain a hold of the yard and maintain a green color. An old work shed sat in the back yard with a cracking piece of cement laid in front of it. A 1971 Plymoth Cuda hardtop stayed on the cement. The Cuda just sat rusting and dirty with a blue tarp covering the front hood of the car screaming, "Please bring me back to life. Return me to the road."

Yellow police tape covered the side door warning people to stay away from the scene. The tape was taken down for a time but was replaced when the case was flagged for a serial killer so that the scene could be reinvestigated. Revan had found that information in the file.

Revan pulled down the tape as he pushed open the side door. The white door looked dirty and beaten. The doorjamb was ripped and broken places where the door knob and deadbolt had lost their grip to remain closed. "The perp kicked in the side door over here." Ray had read the file and the walkthrough of the scene well before Revan had got to work. Ray was the type of person that loathed being late and would be early every time he got the chance. Many times it would be well before anyone else would be even leaving for work. Revan was sure that his ancestors had gotten to the "New World" well before Christopher Columbus. "Mr. James liked to work on old cars in his spare time so they figure that when the perp came in, he grabbed the screw driver from this tool box by the door." He pointed to a toolbox that sat on a table just inside the door with its lid wide open displaying many assorted tools.

The room looked to have a new white paint job with white and grey tile floor. A handmade table looked to be built right into the wall taking up most of the wall leaving only a small bit of room for the boot tray just inside the door. Littering the table with the toolbox were three sets of keys. The boot tray had a muddy pair of brown work boots, a clean pair of white men's running shoes and a pair of black and pink women's tennis shoes. The wall opposite the table held a wall mounted set of coat hooks where a black Carhartt jacket hung by a black women's winter jacket. They all passed through the small area looking around as they did. Ray led the way with Mary bringing up the rear, John was in front of her and Revan behind Ray.

The next room in looked to be a kitchen/dining room as the small group pushed further into the hallway. “Mr. James probably heard the noise and came in the kitchen to see what was going on. The perp was probably on him before he knew what was going on." The kitchen looked to be small but efficient for just one or two people. To their right they were flanked by a cabinet followed by the stove and a counter that wrapped quickly against the wall for the back of the house. In the center of the counter sat a stainless steel sink that was surrounded by a cheap fake marble counter laminate. More cabinet space hung above as far over as the stove. The abrupt end of the counter space was created by an old white fridge.

They all separated looking around and giving each other room. A small dining table sat across the fridge at a short handmade wall bordering the living room. Two simple wooden chairs sat next to the wall where officers and medical personnel moved them out of the way.

The same white and gray tile covered the whole of the kitchen floor.

They all came together to stand around a dried pool of blood on the kitchen tile near the table. Swipes in the blood from when the victim's nerves kept twitching remained along with a few boot prints that led away deeper into the house. Images flashed in Revan's mind as he looked down at the blood seeing the crime scene photos shadowed onto the floor.

James lay spread out on the floor before him dead as an anchor with his grey sweat shirt covered in blood and the chest area tattered from multiple stab wounds. The weapon of choice still protruded out of his neck. His jeans lay lazily on his still legs with a pair of dirty white socks sticking out of the bottom. As Revan still looked upon the image, it slowly faded away showing only the dried blood. Ray looked up at John and saw that he had a queasy look on his face. Everyone then started into the living room that was for the most part together.

The living room was simple and small with an old ugly green carpet that spread over the floor throughout the rest of the house. An old floral print couch sat to the left side of the room across from an average size TV. The TV, cased in black, sat atop a small wood entertainment stand. A small DVD player sat on a shelf below the TV. Two small doors concealed the DVD collection. The team looked quickly at the room and saw that there was nothing of interest and moved on. They turned and walked a short hall to the bedroom, which was a complete mess.

The room was sparse with only an old dresser by the door, a bed next to the far wall and a simple night stand next to it. Across from the bed was a closet door that remained closed while the door into the room was wide open.

The dresser was tipped on its side from the killer rushing into the room after his victim. The night stand lay on the floor with the items that it formally held nearby. A small cheap lamp and old radio alarm clock appeared to be the only items that once stood on the stand. The bed was the area of greatest destruction. A simple bed frame held the box spring in place with the mattress slightly hanging off to the side. A light blue sheet and dark blue comforter lay in a crumpled pile next to the bed next to two white pillows outside of their cases. The mattress looked to have gotten its bottom sheet on before the attack. The sheet was disheveled and stained from a bowel evacuation left behind. A light coating of dust laid on the items in the room from the passing time.

"Ms. Lamon most likely heard her boyfriend being attacked in the kitchen so she tried to hide in here. The killer busted the door in and grabbed the pillowcase off the bed and mercilessly strangled her. Before the killer came here, it looks like the two vics where fixing the bed for a night of staying in. Then after he was done, he just walked right back out and disappeared."

Chapter 5

"Ok, Ray and Mary, I want you to talk with the neighbors and find out if they saw anyone or anything," Revan said. "The person that did this has got to be off his rocker so make sure you ask if there are any locals in town that could fit the bill. I just want to see if we can start to get some names together." They both nodded their heads and headed out of the house to do a quick neighborhood canvas. "John, call the locals and talk with them about anything they have. They know a heck of a lot more about this area than we do so they would have a bit more insight about this. Here's their number from the file." He handed him the number and John made the call on his cell phone. Revan pulled out his cell and made a call to Melissa.

"Melissa, have you heard anything from the others or from the scene techs or the state cops," he asked. He had a thought that he was going to get a bit of bad news.

She said, "The others called and checked in, nothing unusual or new. They did a tour of the scene and are talking to the neighbors and family as we speak. After they're done with that then they're gonna talk with the local cops and head back here." He could hear her messing with some files in the background. "Nothing from the techs but I did talk to the state cops. They said they can't think of anything off hand but they'll get back to us by the end of the week. By the way, the chief said she wants to be briefed at the end of each day by everyone to make sure things are going ok."

As they talked, Revan walked into the kitchen to hear her better. "Ok. Thanks for checking that. We'll be back after we're done here. Tell the chief to quit sweating this, we'll handle things and keep her up to speed on things. Gotta get back to work. Later." Revan hung up the phone and was a bit glad that the state cops didn't have any more bodies to throw on the pile. He turned and saw John walking out of the hallway hanging up his phone.

"The locals have nothing. Nobody has reported anything of interest or out of the ordinary. They only know Ms. Lamon by the fact that she's a recent resident of the area. They don't know whom her family is or how to get a hold of them. The only resident that they say is a bit off is someone they call "One Drink Pete"," John said with a sigh. "But we can take him off the list right now because he was in lock-up at the time of the murders. He was in for walking around town in nothing but his long johns and carrying his 12 gauge shot gun while intoxicated. They still have his gun and only kept him till he sobered up and they dropped him off at home the next day."

Revan leaned against the table and rubbed his chin with his right hand and was just letting the information sink in. Revan stayed there with his eyes closed thinking about all of the information he had been reading and had been told. John wandered about the house seeing if there was anything that he could find that was new to help out the case. An hour passed in that fashion with John turning up nothing and Revan not noticing the time. When John finished, he informed Revan and they both walked outside to see if the other's had returned yet. They both saw Ray and Mary walking up to them from the neighbor's house.

"We got squat, the neighbors didn't see or hear a thing," said Mary. Her pastel blue business suit and blond hair blew in the light breeze. Her business like hair style held firm but the light curls swayed. Her white pumps crunched on gravel as she walked. The only breakup of the light colors that she wore was her badge as it hung over her left breast from the pocket. Long legs flowed down from her short skirt making John stare for a quick moment. Her athletic body gave her a hypnotizing grace as she moved. The only flaw in her good looks was her broken nose.

"The night was slow and relaxing and they turned in early. The next morning they saw the cops head over here and didn't know what was going on until the afternoon. We still got the neighbors on the other side that are also Mr. James' parents. So what do you want us to do now?" Her dark brown eyes locked with John's in a fury as if saying, *"I'm happily married and I'm armed so quit looking at my legs. If I ever catch you looking at my chest, I will shoot you."*

"Alright, we'll all get in the car; we'll head to the morgue to see the bodies our self."

Revan said. "But first we'll stop at his parent's house and get some answers." As they climbed in, Revan held the door for Mary. When everyone was strapped in, Ray pulled out and moved to James' parent's house. When they got there, Ray and Mary got out and headed up to the house to talk with them.

The house was an old two story farm house with a fading white paint job flanked on both sides by trees. Grass was still trying to grow in the yard. The drive way was cracked and had weeds growing willy-nilly. An old Ford pickup sat near the door on the side of the house.

John seemed like he had some questions burning in his brain for Revan to answer. He asked, "Why is it you don't like about me? I'm just here doing my job. I can only do as I'm ordered to by my superiors. I was told not to except a warm reception when I got here, but this is crazy." He seemed to get a bit tenser waiting for Revan to answer him.

"Because I've worked with way too many of you feds before. You guys live, breath, crap, and die by the book," Revan replied in a stern tone. He shifted in his seat to better talk to John by turning to look in the back where John sat behind the driver's seat. "You guys don't relax when doing anything. The only thing you have going with me is the fact that you told me that you were here to observe us. At least you where smart in that aspect. Though I feel that your "superiors" would be a bit pissed if they found out that you told me about that. So if you want to stick around and be some use to me, learn to relax and learn that you have instinct for a reason. Go by it some time, the book was written by people that trusted their instincts."

Revan saw Ray and Mary coming out of the house from the corner of his eye. He turned to sit in the seat comfortably just as they got in the car. "So what do you have for us? Any enemies? How about the girl's family? I hope they know more about her than the cops. And did they see or hear anything?" Mary started to shake her head.

"They're son was well liked by everyone." Ray told. "To their knowledge; he had no enemies at all. Her grandparents immigrated to Texas, her parents died when she was 19 in a tornado so she moved up here." He started up the Jeep and pulled out of the driveway and headed to the morgue. "She has no surviving relatives that they know of. She doesn't have any enemies either. Mr. James usually came over in the morning with Ms. Lamon to visit and have breakfast, when he didn't show up, they headed over to see what was happening and they found the bodies. They called the police immediately. That's all we got. Let's hope that the others had better luck."

The morgue was nowhere near Custer, they drove to Ludington to the Memorial Medical Center. They pulled into the parking lot and piled out of the Jeep. They walked inside and were directed to an examination room to speak with the doctor that handled the bodies. Revan never was much of a fan of trips to the morgue for any reason. It's not that he couldn't stand seeing dead bodies; it was all the boring time there.

The doctor was standing next to a desk looking at papers. The doctor, a middle aged man with graying hair and a white doctor's coat seemed to be humming a little tune to himself. Revan believed that it could be "I'm a little tea pot". His voice sounded as if he was a long time smoker not ready to give it up. On the examination table lay an elderly lady in the stillness of death. He heard them walking in the room.

Revan introduced himself along with his group. The doctor asked what he could do to help them and Revan explained about the case. "Mr. Tea pot" nodded and headed over to a filing cabinet to retrieved the files of the autopsies. He handed them to the group. Revan and Ray looked at James' file while Mary and John looked at Lamon's file. They asked questions about the bodies and the causes of death. John looked like he would be sick but was trying his best to look like he wasn't bothered by the sight of the body.

The doctor told them that James was dead from the first stab, which went through his heart, but the killer just kept going. The killer stabbed using his right hand. James died somewhere between 9:30 pm and 12:30 am. The killer even left the screwdriver in his neck.

Pillowcase used to kill Lamon was still being pulled by the killer after her death. Her windpipe and other parts of her neck were crushed post-mortem with the pillowcase. She died a short while after James on the same day. The times were as close to exact as he could give them. That just told them what they already knew, the killer was sadistic as they come. That and the fact that he was right handed. They all got in the Jeep and headed back to the office.

The others got back a few minutes before them and waited to say hi. They all walked into the office with Melissa still sitting at her desk. "Please tell me you have something that can help me," Revan said as they walked in. Melissa shook her head no with a bit of a sad look on her face. They all sat down at a table in the front of the room. It was the same place that John had been sitting at when Revan showed up to work. The chief walked in as they sat down.

"Ok, what do you have to report?" She questioned. "And I would like to hear some good news so the governor and the holly's will get off my back." She stood there with her hands on her hips waiting for someone to answer her.

"Well, me, Ray, Mary, and John went to Mr. James place and had a look around. We talked to the neighbors and to Mr. James parents. No one had anything useful to add. Ms. Lamon doesn't have any family. Neither had any enemies that anyone knew of as a matter of fact. The locals didn't have anything to add themselves. His parents discovered the bodies after they went to check why they hadn't come over for breakfast that morning. The killer went over kill on both vics. The killer just kicked in the door and killed them both with whatever was on hand for im' to grab. He just kept killing them even after they were dead," Revan explained. "The only thing the M.E. could add is that the killer is right handed. And you guys?" He motioned to the rest of the group.

"Amy, Eric, Derek, and myself went to Miss. Bells house." Barry started. "The killer entered the garage and house through two unlocked doors. The killer came in the kitchen first, grabbed a statue of Zeus off her counter that she got from a trip to Greece, and surprised her pretty well. She ran into the living room where he beat her to death with the statue. Her neighbor and best friend Mrs. Johnson found the body when she was checking why she didn't show up to lunch with her. Like the first two vics, he kept beating her after she was dead. She passed between 7:30 pm and 11:00pm. The locals there didn't have anything to add either. Her kids were with their dad for the weekend because of the divorce a year before hand. Her other neighbors didn't have anything for us. The M.E. there gave us the same info about the killer being right handed."

Melissa spoke up, "Revan asked me to get a hold of the state police to see if they had any cases or information to add. They didn't know of anything off hand but said they would check and get back with us by the end of the week. The fingerprints left behind at both scenes are a match, the shoe prints are a match also. They will also let us know if the DNA is a match. They say that so far, it looks like there is only one killer that is doing this. So we have what looks like a right-handed killer that wears size 12 1/2 work boots. They'll get back to us on the brand of boots he wears. That's all that they have so far."

The chief said blowing out a breath, "Alright, well at least it's a start. This may get the governor off my case for the rest of the day. I hope that you have more tomorrow." She left the room not quite happy but at least she wasn't mad about the little bit of information. Revan knew she would be all over them the next day.

"Alright guys, anything to add that you didn't want to tell her," Revan inquired. Everyone shook their head no. "Ok, well finish up your paper work and have a good day. But let's hope that tomorrow we have better luck and we find this psycho soon. I really don't want to have to deal with much more of this lunatic's over kill scenes."

Chapter 6

They were only a week into the investigation and things were going nowhere fast. The only thing good anyone had was that the guy hadn't struck again. Revan could only hope that something would turn up that wasn't a body. They did find out that the killer wore Caterpillar work boots though, the same pair at all scenes. This information played in Revan's mind over and over again along with the rest of the information.

After his normal four and a half hours sleep, he woke up in the darkness of the morning. He put on his work out cloths and spent an hour exercising. He ate a breakfast of eggs, toast, and fresh fruit. Afterwards he stripped his clothes off and took a hot shower. Gazing into the mirror as he toweled off, he looked at the scar on his chest. It was an ugly white scar that went diagonally from the left down to the right. Situated over his heart; it was a constant memory like the others; of the former friend that turned on him and left him for dead. A number of other scars that ranged from cuts, to bullet holes, to fire and even electricity held their place on various parts of his body.

He got dressed and headed for the office. He decided to take his black 99' BMW 7-series E38 because of the weather. The news said it could rain and with the way Michigan is with weather, you never knew. He wore blue jeans, black skater shoes, a light blue hoodie, a black leather jacket and his baseball cap backwards.

On the way he kept trying to think if there was something that they over looked. The only thing that was good that past week was that the last night Melissa and he went to the movies and to dinner. They went out as friends. Revan took her out to repay her for the work she was doing and the hard work he knew was gonna be ahead of her and the rest of them. He pulled into the parking lot and was pissed.

A TV news van was sitting in the lot with a reporter hanging out. Revan knew that he couldn’t get away from the guy without catching heck. The reporter, a young guy that looked like all he would get was the crap assignments walked up to him. He had a charcoal grey suit on and was playing with his hair for the camera. He motioned for his camera lady to follow him. She was wearing khaki pants and top with her hair hidden under a Tigers hat. She lifted the camera on her shoulder and got her shot of both Revan and the reporter. The reporter hammered Revan with questions about the case and the investigation unit. Revan talked through the interview keeping as much information to himself that he could. He didn't want many details about the case in the press that would create copycat killers. The reporter thanked him and left with a sulk knowing he got next to nothing from Revan.

Revan walked inside just as it started to rain. It looked like the weather people were right for once. The news reporter had been waiting for him or anyone because he couldn't get inside the building. Revan had made sure that no one could get in without someone knowing it. A special ID tag was given to all personnel and they were tracked very carefully. As he walked the hall he started to get a bad feeling. He thought; "*man do I hope I'm wrong about this feeling.*" He walked into the office. It was just Derek, Melissa, and himself.

"Well if it isn’t the best part of my day," Revan said to Melissa raising his hand. "Did you have fun?" She smiled and nodded her head. Files and paperwork were on her desk that she was filling out. “How’s your knee?" Before she could answer him, the phone rang. He let her answer it.

"So what did you do last night?" Derek inquired. His suit twisted tight over his athletic body as he turned his body to face Revan. The old white scar on the bridge of his nose was still visible even against his white skin. "Did you and Melissa go out last night? Can we start calling you two an item?"

"Yes we went out," Revan said sitting down at the table with Derek. He looked at him and thought that he was made for Fraud work. His slicked back black hair, stern black eyes, and suits helped make him look the part. Being in his early 30s also played into the look. "We went to a movie then out to eat. Yes we had fun and no you guys can't start calling us an item. We are just two friends that went out for fun."

"Right, right, right," Derek rebutted. "And that little conversation you two just had or were about to have was just friends. And how many friends greet each other with "Well if it isn't the best part of my day?"" He sat back in his chair feeling like he had Revan at that point, which to a degree he did. Revan and Melissa had talked about seeing each other again but had decided to mainly stay as friends with a chance at dating again. Before Derek and Revan could really get into the argument, the others showed up.

They all said there hellos to one another and Melissa got off the phone. She had a look of absolute dread on her face. Revan knew the day was going to be a bad day. "That was the state police. We have another murder," she said. "This time, it's a family. It's on John Street in Bad Axe. George Samson, 39, Pam Samson, 37, Lisa Samson, 17, and Ben Samson, 10." Everyone was struck with shock and disgust. Everyone just sat back to catch our breath and collect our selves. Hearing about another murder from this killer was bad enough but throwing in a kid made it so much worse. "It's about 4 hours away. If you want to make it back here before night, you should go. They're waiting for you. But the way, George Samson, there is something you need to know." They all turned grimly at her. "He was a cop."

Revan kick a chair into the wall in his frustration. "Let’s go," he said with a growl. "John, I need you to stay here, get a hold of the FBI’s labs and find out what they have. Let’s hope they know who he is and that he doesn't have a grave yard behind him." John got up and grabbed the files with prints from Melissa. He headed down to the labs for a copy of the DNA sequence to send to the FBI that they had just received. The rest of them walked out to their cars a bit somber and a bit angry. Nothing hurt as bad as hearing about a family being murdered but it hurt more when it's a cop and his family. Barry and Amy rode with Revan. Eric, Ray, Mary rode with Derek.

The three of them rode in silence the whole way. Revan took I-96 to I-69 heading east pushing the BMW as hard as he could. From I-69, he hopped onto M-53 headed north right to Bad Axe. It was the longest ride Revan has had in his life. He pulled on to John Street; it was still filled with police cars and people wondering what was going on. The whole look made the group wonder why it was still so busy. The neighborhood looked like it should have been an average place that kids could grow up care free.

The holly's were all jockeying for the best place to get some images of the house and bodies. Trying their best to get anything they could from the officers at the scene. Revan and Derek had to park almost a block away. They all got out of the cars and walked up to the scene. It was still raining lightly but it looked like it would clear up. Revan was thanking god that the holly's didn't recognize them and start bugging them for information. He had had enough of that for one day. A police officer still in his rain gear stopped them for only a second till they showed their badges. Revan walked up to a state trooper that looked like he is in charge. He put out his hand to shake. The officer reached out and shook Revan's. "This is one heck of a bad day to meet. I'm Lieutenant Revan Lygar of the Michigan Serial Killer

Investigation Unit," Revan said.

"Yeah same here." he said. After hearing Revan's name, he raised an eyebrow for a second. "I'm Captain Briggs of the local state police post." He was a bigger guy, a bit over weight with grey hair sticking out from under his hat. He wore the standard dark blue state trooper uniform covered in a dark blue rain slicker. He managed to pull off a look of being sad and outright pissed at the same time. "I'm sure you're wondering why we called you. We saw the news about the other murders and when we were called about this, we thought it may belong to your guy," he said in a horse voice. "Are the fingerprints from the other scenes in the system?"

Revan nodded his head yes. He had the feeling that this was the work of their man too.

"Ok, then if this is the guy, we should hear from the lab and know if this is your guy. Either way, I feel that this is yours." Briggs' phone rang and he pulled it out to look at it. "Well speak of the devil. That's the lab now. I gave them a rush order to get the prints checked. Give me a second." He answered his phone and

Revan started to mosey on over to the garage. After a moment of conversation he came up behind Revan. "Yeah, it's your guy alright. I had the techs run the prints as soon as they found them. Would you like a walkthrough of the scene?" Revan nodded yes again.

He started his walkthrough. "Well as I'm sure you have been told, George Samson was a fellow officer. He was a state trooper himself. He had today off so he had a tee time at the golf-course like he always has once a week even when it rains," he said. "We're pretty sure the killer started around 10:00, 10:15 pm last night. George was probably out here cleaning and checking his clubs for today."

The garage sat at the end of a black top driveway. The door wide open showing the inside of the garage blanketed in yellow light. The area of greatest concern was the workbench on the left side of the garage with blood splattered all around and a pool spread across the floor. The garage stood separate from the house with the only link being a small walkthrough fence to the backyard. The house sat next to the driveway with a door leading out to the driveway. The house had a white paint job with a brown trim that was shared with the garage. In the driveway sat a red 2000 Toyota Camry Solara with its trunk standing open showing golf bag half full of clubs. The bag and the inside of the truck was soaked from the rain.

"We figure that the killer came in the open garage door and grabbed a club out of his trunk. He beat George badly. But he killed him by strangling him with the club. The ME says that if he hadn't been strangled, he would have died from his injuries anyway. After he was strangled, the lunatic started beating him again," Briggs stated as they walked into the garage. Outside of the crime scene area, the garage was neat and tidy. Tools and other items for the upkeep of the yard hung in an orderly manner over the walls and on selves. By the workbench were evidence tags spread around variously, sitting mainly around the blood splatters. The bodies had already been taken away for processing well before the team arrived.

Revan asked a few questions about the state of the scene and the victim as he looked around. After a minute of walking around, Revan and Briggs walked out of the garage towards the side door of the house.

"Mrs. Samson was inside washing dishes from what we can tell and probably heard the ruckus and came to see what was going on. She saw her husband being killed and ran inside to protect her son Ben who was asleep upstairs in his bedroom." They walked inside past a kitchen to the living room.

They were standing just inside the living room looking at a small bloodstain at the bottom of the stairs with more evidence tags. The floor under the blood was a highly polished hard wood floor that refused to soak up the blood. The stair case was the same type and color wood as the floor. The living room looked undisturbed outside of the blood by the stairs and the smashed lamp nearby. The living room was lightly decorated with pictures of a happy family. The main items in the room were a large flat screen TV against the far wall with a brown couch across from it. The smashed lamp looking like it had no place to go in the living room. Looking down a hallway to another part of the house; Revan wondered how far the killing had spread.

"The killer followed her inside and caught her at the top of the stairs. He struggled with her for a second and threw her down the stairs. Her neck broke on the way down. But the killer dropped a heavy lamp off a table down on top of her. Man, this guy is sick," Briggs said taking off his hat and wiping his brow.

They walked up the stairs stepping carefully trying to avoid disturbing any evidence. The hallway at the top of the stairs went from the front of the house to the back of the house. Two doors were set off to the front and two off to the back leading to other rooms. The hallway was laid with hard wood floor and a hallway rug running the length of the area. A few small tables stood against the walls with decorations sitting on each one. More pictures hung from the walls. One table sat near the stairs but its few decorations such as picture frames lay on the floor nearby. The biggest decoration was missing, the lamp used to finish off Mrs. Samson.

"Ben most likely heard his mom and

woke up from the commotion. He probably started to ask for him mom and the killer heard him." They walked down the hall towards the back of the house. They headed for one doorway that stood wide open. They moved into a small bedroom that looked like a kid's room.

A red racecar bed sat off to the right side of the room with a superhero comforter pulled off to lay at the end of the bed like a forgotten memory. A small table serving as a desk sat against the wall opposite the bed. Along the far wall sat a wooden toy box and a small book shelf full of various books.

"The sick sucker smothered him with his own pillow. He pushed down so hard down on Ben's face that he broke his nose. He fought back and ended up biting a hole in the pillow but didn't save him." He hung his head trying to hold back tears and said, "Ben would have been 11 next week."

Revan's phone rang. "Excuse me, it's the office," he said. Briggs nodded his head happy that he would have a moment to collect himself. Revan stepped out into the hallway. "Yeah

Melissa, what do ya got for me."

She replied, "I just got another call for the state police. They just got done checking through their cases and came up empty. At least that is some good news. How are things over there?"

"More bodies and names to add to the list. This guy is pretty sick," he said looking at the ground hoping in the back of my mind that it was all a bad dream. "Has the lab gotten back on the DNA?"

"Yeah they have." she answered. "It's a positive match. There is only one killer. Blood type A positive and we have his DNA profile as well. One sec, John handed me a paper. Ok, uh huh. Well the FBI doesn't have anything. At least nothing that can be tied to our guy but they promise to get back with us after they do more checking."

"Thanks, let me know if anything comes up," he said. Revan hung up the phone and turned towards Capt. Briggs. "Sorry about that. The DNA came back. It looks like we only have one killer on our hands and he's our problem. The FBI didn't come up with anything either.

Can we continue, and who found the bodies?"

Briggs replied gathering his breath, "The guy who lives across the street. When he woke up and saw the garage door open he started to come over to find out why, he saw George laying on the ground in a pool of blood. He ran back to his house and called 911. Anyway Ben wasn't his last one. He looked to be heading out of the house when he got another one." They walked down stairs to the kitchen.

The kitchen was a generous size. Dark stained wooden cabinets on the floor and along the ceiling. A black stove sat off to the left side with a small cabinet area to its left by the door to the backyard. A microwave sat on the counter along with other kitchen implements place across the counter that looked like they had gotten pushed around. On the wall that lined the drive way there were cabinets with a sink placed in the middle of the counter. A dish drainer once sat to the right of the sink. The drainer and it's last set of drying dishes lay on the grey stone laminate tile floor by the cabinets. Most of the drainer's former occupants lay across the floor with the plates broken. A few dirty dishes sat on the left of the sink still waiting to feel the soap and water. The sink looked to still have water in it but it was the wrong color. Away from the kitchen at the edge towards the living room sat the dining room table. The table looked to be cherry wood with a matching set of chairs.

Briggs had Revan follow him to the sink. As they looked in, Revan finally saw what was wrong with the water; it was pink from blood. A few half clean dishes sat in the blood water like it was soap. "Lisa came home from a friend's house around 10:30 pm. She most likely saw her father in the garage and came inside to call 911. She then most likely saw her mom dead by the stairs. She went to call 911 but the killer was still here and surprised her. He drowned her in the sink. He slammed her head so hard in the sink that her head broke a plate and split her head wide open." Revan could see Briggs face shift to utter disgust. "Sorry, I got a kid of my own her age. In fact they were friends and it was my house that she was coming home from last night." He paused trying to hold back tears. After a moment, he managed to continue. "These things you never get use to. I hope that we get this lunatic soon. I think people like this are the reason for the death penalty. Too bad we don't have one. I wonder if Texas will lend us one for a little while."

He showed Revan outside to talk some more while the scene techs finished processing the house. It had stopped raining but the clouds were still gloomy and overcast. "So have you talked to the neighbors and family yet?" Revan questioned. He was hoping for some good news but he knew better the moment it came out of his mouth.

"We talked to the entire neighborhood on this road and his family," the captain reported. "No one saw anything or anyone unusual. No one in the family had enemies. Least not any obvious enemies outside the type that any cop gets. We'll send the evidence to your labs. I hope that he gets to see the inside of cell so we can all tell him how we feel in court. I'll have my office send you copies of the paper work." They shook hands and Revan went to meet up with the others. The look of relief on Briggs face helped lighten Revan's heart. He knew that it tore Briggs heart to have to do the walkthrough.

Amy had been talking to the ME who had came back to talk with them. She walked over to tell him what she had. “The ME told me that like the others, he went over kill with the vics." she reported. The former Marine brushed away her dark brown hair from her face. The moved hair revealed the scar on her left jaw and the two on the left side of her neck. "Mr. Samson was hit nearly 50 times before he was strangled and beat some more. One of the hits was so hard to his back it fractured a few of his vertebrae. He would have died without being choked. Mrs. Samson's neck broke when she went down the stairs. The lamp broke two ribs, one punctured her lung. Either way, she was a goner. Ben was smothered so hard, it broke his nose. They also found some stuffing from pillow in his throat. When Lisa's head hit the dish, it knocked her unconscious but the killer kept slamming her head in the sink. Her skull was cracked and broken from the hits. These poor kids deserved better than this. This guy is a real sick-o. The ME's office will fax copies of the papers to our office."

"The state troopers are going to send us theirs also." Revan said. The others came over to see what was new. Revan talked just loud enough for group to hear him but no one else. The last things that he felt they needed was for a reporter to over hear their conversation."Don't say anything to the press, I want tight lips. You guys know your contracts. Let's get back to the office, we have more names to add to the file and see what else we can come up with." They all went back to the cars in the same groups they showed up in.

The ride back was as equally silent as the ride over. Revan just kept running the scene and the facts through his head and the violence exhibited at each scene. There was no pattern to what the guy was doing. He only killed, and at random. There was no link between any of the victims. His only pattern was that he killed everyone inside. That was the only thing that could be expected when they got called to a scene; that everyone would be dead. He would go over kill. They just didn't like the facts because it was all they had. They had fingerprints, blood, hair, and boot prints but other than that, they had known squat. This guy was really starting to piss him off.

They got back to the office late. The chief was waiting for them in the office with Melissa and John. "How bad is it?" she inquired to Revan. He could only give her a look of utter despair. "Melissa told me what she knows. How about you fill in the rest?"

Revan walked to the table and sat down in a chair. He put his elbows on his knees and rested his chin against his fists. He let out a sigh and started his report. "We have four more bodies to bury and four more names to add to the list; a cop, his wife, his young son, and his teenage daughter. We have fingerprints and blood but no name to give to his identity. He's racking up bodies and we ain't got nothin'. The state police and the ME said they would send us copies of the reports as soon as their done. All evidence is being forwarded to our lab. The FBI has nothing either. It looks like we're up a creek without a paddle. I hate to admit it, but we may need to do a press conference. Hopefully we can get some leads and get somewhere out of this pit of crap. But I'm not doing it. I'll show up but I'm not talking."

"Alright, I'll arrange the press conference for tomorrow afternoon. You better show up," she said pointing at Revan with a frown. "At least the holly's will be happy. They have been bugging me all day about this case. You don't have to talk but at least dress up a little. Look like you have some professional sense." With that said, she left the room to start making calls. Her parting thought was that maybe the next day would be better.

"Alright everyone, finish your work and go home," Revan told everyone. "Be ready for tomorrow, it looks like we'll be answering phones all day."

They each left the room slowly lost in thought. After reaching each of their offices, they tried to prepare for the following day knowing that the calls would pour in.

Chapter 7

Revan left the press conference not happy about having to deal with the holly's and his suit. He knew his time would be better suited going through leads rather than standing around. The conference took place in the press room. It was a large room with many folding chairs and a podium. The unique part of the room was the doors. A set of doors that led outside were just key lockable so that the press could come and go. The other doors were locked like the main entrance doors so that the press could not get in the main building.

He entered the office to phones ringing. "God, I frickin' hate ties," he grumbled. He started to tear at his tie. As he walked to his office to help answer calls, Melissa passed him a file with a list of leads. A runner was going around to the offices and rooms retrieving the lists of leads and bringing them to Melissa to hold for Revan.

The only thought that he had was that it was going to be a long difficult day. The state troopers and some of the local police that had the day off volunteered their time to help answer calls. They occupied a few of the extra offices in the building. He tore off the tie and threw it on his desk leaving his door open to the outer office. His cell phone rang as he sat down; he didn't completely recognize the number outside of it being a state police number.

"Revan, this is Captain Briggs," he said sounding a bit rushed. "As soon as the press conference was over we started to get some calls. We're working on the leads as we speak. There's quite a few calls but we'll sort through em'. But I did get a strange call that I wanted to call you about."

"Alright, shoot," Revan replied. He sat in his chair thumbing through the folder Melissa handed him. He could see John headed to his office with another folder for him.

Briggs started, "Well, a lady called saying that the James/Lamon murders were not the killers first, a murder in Pellston came before. She wouldn't say how long before. I just got off the phone with the state police branch up near there. Their going through the case files up there and will get back with me if they come up with anything. But I'm sure you're getting the same feeling that I'm getting from this."

He was right. Revan put the folder down and ran his fingers through his hair. "Ok. Thanks for letting me know. By the way, did you get any information on the informant so we can try and talk to her? It would be nice to find out how she knew about any other murders. Call me if you get anything else or a call from them," he said.

“No I didn’t get any info. We tried a trace and came up with a pay phone in Nashville Tennessee on a busy as corner. There is not a snow ball’s chance in heck at figuring out who the heck was on the phone,” Briggs said. “The best info I got for you is that she sounded like she smoked a lot to me. All we can hope now is that maybe she will call back and we can her to talk more. No matter what, I will give you a call when I have something. Talk to you later.” They both hung up their phones.

The calls tapered off about two hours after they began. The whole unit was worn out from the number they received. Revan knew that a number of the calls would come up worthless but as an officer of the law, every lead needed to be run to the end. They ended up with around 3000 leads but maybe only 20 to 30 of them would be worthwhile if they had any luck. That number was just the calls that came into their office.

Revan called his unit to his office to discuss the leads. He divided the leads up so they all had some to start, a bit over 300 per person. He told everyone to sort through and find the ones that seemed most promising and list them out. Melissa helped to make some calls to state police to check out leads.

As Revan sat down at his desk, his phone rang again but he recognized the number that time. Capt. Briggs said as he answered the phone, "Hey Revan. I just wanted to check in. The other state police post hasn't called back yet. It may just turn out to be nothing." He sounded more relaxed that time, probably because the calls were winding down. "A few of the leads you sent our way have been checked and are nothing special."

"Ok, thanks for letting us know," Revan

said. "By the way, how in the heck did you get my number?"

"When I got the call, I figured best if I talk to you directly and so I called over there and your chief gave me your number," Briggs replied. "She wasn't happy that I wanted you but after I explained the call to her, she caved in and gave me your number."

"Alright, get back to us as soon as you hear back about the call. You know I'm gonna have to hear about this crap for a week or so. Thanks again," Revan said as he hung up. He wanted to have another talk to his team so he had Melissa call them to the outer office.

He looked around the room at everyone. He leaned against the wall to his office as he addressed them. "Alright everyone," he announced. They stopped talking amongst themselves to listen. "So far this case is on a level of suck all new and we aint got nothin'. If you got contacts anywhere, talk to them. Find out if there is anyone that they can help point us to. We have all the evidence in the world against this guy but no name or face to stick it to. I'm gonna head out and see if I can scare up anything useful myself. I want you all to take it easy; we're gonna get this guy." He said his goodbyes after he locked his office to leave.

When he got outside, a few reporters were waiting in the lot. The reporters were the ones that stayed behind from the conference. The others had already gathered up their cables and cameras and left. The ones that stayed were careful to avoid the doors. The signs that said "no press allowed" was clearly posted. They had been warned before the press conference that they were only allowed in the building when invited. They whined about it but kept their distance. As Revan stepped outside, the reporters bothered him with more questions. He told them that any questions would be answered in press releases or future press conferences. They whined even more but he got in his car and left.

He still had a bunch of people that he knew when he was young that he could get a hold of. In his last job he kept close ties with a number of them as they spread out across the state and the country. Many of them were in different lines of work that were useful back then and could still be useful. With the change of jobs, he had not talked to his contacts in a while. It wouldn't take him long to make the calls and go see people but he needed to get his feelers out. He jumped into his BMW listening to Three Days Grace "World so cold" and headed home so he could change out of his monkey suit.

Changed and showered, he sat at his table in the dining room and started to peruse through his contact books to start looking for a good start point. Revan owned a two story house just where he wanted it. He bought 50 acres past North Muskegon that was all woods. He cleared about an acre square in the middle of it and built his dream house, a two story house with a basement. The basement was furnished so that two thirds was a game and rec-room. The rest was his office. He put his library on the main floor along with the standard rooms of a house. He loved the house and was happy with it. A two car garage housed his BMW and his 96' Dodge Viper. A small look-a-like barn was build off to the side of the back yard to house his motorcycle and his favorite car, his 1969 Dodge Charger that he had fully restored outside of some aftermarket parts that gave it some more horses.

He walked to the fridge and got a Mountain Dew and started thumbing through numbers and names at the table on his phone. The kitchen had grey marble counter tops set on top of oak cabinets. A stove took up part of the space on the far wall and a sink sat in the counter on the adjoining wall. An island sat in the middle of the kitchen. A stainless steel fridge sat in the wall opposite the sink next to the door into the pantry. The portion of the counter opposite the stove created a slight wall between the kitchen and the dining room. The floor in the kitchen and the dining room was dark hard wood flooring. The walls of both rooms were painted white. In the middle of the dining room sat a dining table with four matching chairs. The wall behind the table had a sliding glass door to the patio deck and backyard.

He wrote down some names he figured that would yield some information. A combination of doctors, drug dealers and other illegal professions that some of his friends had become.

He took the folders and headed to his office. The office was a decent size one and a good place to work alone. The office sat at the far end of the basement from the stairs. The basement was completely finished with gaming posters covering the walls not occupied by the book selves. A desk took up one wall and another wall held a few book shelves. The book shelves were crammed with various books on law and misc jobs in law enforcement. The shelf in the middle was only half full though. On the right hand side was just a picture frame, a face from his past. A young woman he knew many years ago. Every time he looked at the picture, he remembered her those years ago and a promise to himself and her. A promise to find out why and who did it.

He sat and started making lists on paper.

List one; Scene 1

-Northern Michigan

-Two people in the house

-Both killed with weapons at hand

-Over use of force for death
-Stabbing and strangulation was used
List two; Scene 2
-Southwest Michigan
-One person in house
-Killed with weapon at hand
-Over use of force for death
-Blunt force trauma was used
List three; Scene 3
-Eastern Michigan
-Three people in house
-Killed with weapons at hand
-One person comes home
-Killed with weapon at hand
-Over use of force for death
-Blunt force trauma, strangulation, suffocation, and blunt force trauma were used
List 4; Killer
-Kills everyone in building
-Uses anything he can get his hands on
-Goes over board and continues to harm body after death
-Leaves DNA, leaves finger prints, leaves hair, leaves boot prints
-Right handed, blood type A positive, size 12

1/2 Caterpillar work boots

-Strikes at different places across state

-Is completely nuts

He made the few calls he could and got the word out but otherwise came up with nothing.

Chapter 8

Revan decided to take a drive and clear his head before he went back to the office to talk with the chief. He took the BMW and headed for downtown to see how things were turning out with all the construction that was happening. He drove down 120 onto 31as it turned into Shoreline drive. As he got off Shoreline drive and he turned toward L.C. Walker Arena. He kept driving past just wandering around random streets. As he drove north on 1st street and came to Seaway drive, he saw a book store in a small strip mall and decided to see what they had for sale.

He wanted to see if they had any good mystery books and anything else that might perk his interest. There was only one car in the lot and he figured that it belong to whoever was working. The building it occupied was older and looked inviting for the small store. The name was painted in big red letters that hung from a wooden sign just behind the glass, "Miss Heather's books and poems". He thought back and remembered someone else that went by that name but set it aside and walked inside and the all too familiar chime sounded. He could see that half the store held books but the other half was poetry, just as the sign promised. Revan started to look through the books. He was wandering towards the poems when he heard someone in the back of the store.

"Just a minute," a voice called from the back. The voice sounded familiar. One he hadn't heard in years. She came out from the back with a small stack of books in her hands. She stopped when she saw his face. "Is that you? Oh my god, I can't believe that's you," she said as she dropped the books on the floor. Now that she stood there in front of him, he couldn't believe it was her.

The beautiful young woman in front of him was a friend he hadn't seen since she helped him track a murderer. "Heather Lawrence. I never thought I would see you again," Revan said as he walked up to her to give her a big hug. He first met her about four years prior when she was called in to help his group track a killer. Her brown eyes still looked hypnotic. "So what the heck have you been up to sense the poetic killer," he asked her hugging her again.

She gave him a light sharp punch to the stomach. "I was worried sick after you left you jerk," she said with her hands on her hips under her casual clothing. The stud in her upper lip on the right shined in the sun light. "I tried to find out but no one knew where the heck you went. I understand that the work you were doing is important but you left without a word. The least you could have done was write a letter or call to let me know you were alright. I almost gave up on you. I thought I would never see you again. At least you seem like you are able to keep your promises."

Revan was holding his stomach acting like it hurt a little said, "I'm sorry, I had to take care of things. I needed to head back to work to finish what I started and find a way out of my job so I made up my mind and left. I figured if I made it out alive that I would need some where to start in life and seeing you would be a good start. But after I was done..." Revan let out a sigh, groping for the right thing to say. "I got in a bit over my head and didn't want to drag you into it. So I thought best to let you be and live your life."

"So you were thinking of breaking that promise? You were just going to leave me worrying about you," she questioned him. She let out a short breath and gave him a hug and said, "Well at least you did come back." She let go of him so they could talk. "I saw you on the news earlier where they were talking about some killer. You looked like you didn't want to be there. What the heck is going on?"

"It's a long story about a really sick person," he explained. "How about we get together for dinner and talk? If you really want to know, I'll tell you then. But I really need to get back to the office. My chief will be jumping down my throat if I don't give her report before I knock off for the day." He wrote on a piece of paper and handed it to Heather. "This is my address and cell number, how about we get together around six?"

Heather took the paper and said, "Ok, I'll see you around six. I'll call if I'm going to be late. And sense when did you ever care about anyone that has a higher position than you?"
Revan shrugged as he headed out the door. There was nothing he could say. He went to the

office and gave the chief what little debrief there was to give. He headed to the store so he could see what he could make for dinner. He couldn't help but to have a lighter step having seen Heather. He hadn't seen her in a little over 3 years and she looked just as good when he saw her as she did when he last seen her.

Chapter 9

The weather was slowly getting better. He slowly walked past some storefront windows. The store he was passing had many TV's in the window. Some were big and the rest were small, but they all were turned to the same station. What was playing at the moment, he couldn't help but to stop and watch. It was a press conference of some kind. A woman in a dark blue business suit and black hair that was just starting to grey stood behind a podium with a government type symbol on the front. Off to the side was a young man in a dark suit and looked like he'd rather be anywhere but there. He had a scar that went vertically down through his right eye and one that crossed his left cheek. A look of danger seemed to surround him.

"Good morning ladies and gentlemen," she started. "My name is Chief Beth Waterfurd and this is Lieutenant Revan Lygar of the Michigan Serial Killer Investigation Unit." She gestured to the young man next to her. "We are calling on the public for any information about a killer that is loose in the state. The killer to date has 7 victims. The killer struck in Custer on

South Main Street, in Eastmont on Cutter parkway southeast, and in Bad Axe on John Street. Anyone who may have seen the killer near the scene of the crime is urged to call the police with any information they have. So far the killer seems to show up on foot and wears size 12 1/2 work boots to the scene. He uses items at the scene to kill. The killer would have been covered in blood after the killings. We have yet to find a logical pattern for the killings. We urge everyone to make sure that you doors and windows are securely locked. Don't let anyone into your home that you do not know and are unsure of. Once again, anyone with information is urged to call police. Thank you." The press in the room went into a flurry asking questions and taking pictures.

He stared at the TV's for a long while and slowly started to come back to the world. He could only think in shifting thoughts. "So it's just now starting to catch up," he said to himself in a low voice. He no longer called himself by his name. He had lived with the pulse so long that it felt that he was one with it. He called himself the Pulse to be more in touch with it.

"Well Pulse, what to do now? Do we wait till we move again or continue our work here? No, we're not waiting till then again. We continue the work."

Pulse got back to his motel room a few hours later. He sat on his bed so he could think. "This doesn't change a thing. I'm the pulse. Nothing can stop the pulse. Tonight I have work to do. I can feel it." He grabbed his bag from under the bed and made sure everything was in its place. The dark pulse started again. "Hmm. I've never felt it this strong this early. But it knows when to do the job." He got on his boots and his new clothes. The boots were always the same but the cloths were from a small thrift store he found. The thrift store cloths helped in keeping the money cheap and always having new cloths for his work.

He walked around town. His medium length brown hair moved in the breeze. The dark pulse sent him here and there past houses and stores. As he walked past a store, it hit him hard. Time to do the job. He saw no cars in the lot, strange for the late afternoon. He shrugged it off and stepped inside. The store was a candle shop, the kind that you see a lot of hippies and yuppies in he thought. The smell of the store was strong with flowers and fruits.

Rows of candles sat on many shelves allowing their fragrances fill the air. All of the shelves were wooden looking like they were made in someone's backyard. The counter with the register was off to the left of the door. The counter was a glass one that has some smaller candles and incense lining the shelves inside. The cash register was white that was dulling and getting dirty. Behind the counter were more shelves with even more candles. On the lower shelf sat a few candles that were lit. Hanging behind the counter on the far wall was a tie-dye curtain that served as a make shift door to the back.

He could hear someone in the back of the shop. He looked around to see what he could use. He picked up a larger candle that was in a glass jar. It was heavy; just what he needed. He felt that it was ironic that this person worked in a candle shop and that he was going to kill them with a candle.

He maneuvered around the counter and headed to the back room. As he pushed past the side of the curtain, he saw her bending over looking into a box filled with different colored candles. She was old, had to have been 80 he thought. She was heavier than she had to be. Her grey hair was done up in a pony-tail against her black skin tone. She wore a bright pink shirt and tie-dye skirt.

Pulse raised the candle above his head as she turned to see him. When she laid her eyes on him, her face went from a calm business like demeanor to fear. She saw the candle and knew what was going to happen. As he brought the candle down, she raised her hands in defense but it was too late. He hit her on the left temple of her head. She fell to the ground out of her chair. He was rising to strike again as she fell. When she hit the ground, he was bringing the candle down again. He hit her on the side of her head and felt her skull give away. He hit again and again till he was out of strength. The candle left in his hand was less than half there. Pieces laid on the ground around her head and imbedded in her face. What was left of her face looked like a pile of ground meat. He stood back to look at what he had done. He dropped the candle on the floor.

His thoughts turned to leaving. Pulse looked around. Which way to go? It was the middle of the day. He took off his over shirt and turned it inside out and wrapped it around his waist. The blood from killings was the reason that he made sure he wore a second shirt. He looked at his pants and saw that the black grey color was hiding the few drops of blood that landed on them. With the blood covered, it was time to leave. He calmly walked out from the back and headed to the front door. He stopped and looked around to make sure no one was around. Seeing no one, he pushed open the door and headed down the street walking with complete calm.

He got back to his room still calm and cool. He stripped out of his cloths and jumped into the shower. Like always, he took it freezing cold. When he was done, he changed into fresh clothes and started cutting the death clothes into small strips. By the time he was done, he had a pile of clothing that needed taking care of. Dark started to fall and it was time to finish. He looked out his door and found the metal trash can he had been moving closer to his door for the last few days. No one was around so he grabbed it and brought it into his room. Pulse spent the rest of the night burning the strips one at a time so the fire alarms wouldn't be set off. It took three hours to burn them all, he brought the trash can back outside and placed it back where it started off. He stripped his clothes off and climbed into bed. His hand rested on his flat stomach glad that he had lost that weight from college.

Morning; Pulse woke up refreshed and ready to get going. He gathered his things and made sure nothing was missing. He put the bags into the car and headed to the manager's office to turn in the key. "I'm Mr. Dranns checking out of room 7," Pulse said to the old manager that was busy watching TV. He slid the key under the window. Pulse stayed at motels that only asked for a name and cash down for how long you would be around. He used his real name at the motel knowing that if the police started checking around that they would start with names that were fake.

"Ok, thanks for stayin' Mr. Dranns," the old guy said. "Have you seen the TV lately?" Pulse nodded his head. "That new police unit has been on talkin' about the loon ball that has been killing people. The news keeps showing the same press conference over and over but hasn't said anything new. Yeash, the cops sit there and say they have all this evidence against the killer but they don't know who he is or even what he looks like. Cryminy. Just another waste of taxpayer money." He turned away from his TV to address Pulse for the first time. "Alright, well here's your receipt. Thanks again for stayin'." The old man handed Pulse a slip that stated how long he stayed and how much it cost him. He pocketed the slip for paperwork later. With that done, he got into his car and headed out for somewhere new to continue his work. He knew that his pulse would always have work for him.

Chapter 10

Revan was still in the kitchen grabbing the last few things for dinner when there was a knock at the door. He opened the door to Heather looking lovely as ever. He wore a grey shirt he got that he felt made him look like a prep but it was comfortable and a pair of dark blue jeans, she wore a black v-neck shirt and black pants that matched. The whole set helped show how good of a body she had despite what she and others tended to think. She left her hair down and it still flowed just below her shoulders and she was wearing the black eyeliner. She left her upper lip piercing in to sparkle in the light.

"Well hello beautiful," Revan said stepping aside for her to come inside. He was doing his best he thought to keep her from ripping his head off again by getting back to how he talked to her before he had left. "Please come on in." He thought that with how long it took him back then to start getting her use to being called beautiful. Did she go back to thinking that she's not good looking? God I hope not he thought, but if she did, why not start arguing about that again. There are worse things to fight about in this world.

"I had a little trouble finding your place but as you can see, I'm not still out there looking," she said. Her eyes took in the room as she said, "It's a great place, you own it?"

"Yup, it's all mine. 50 acres and this house I designed myself. Dinner is ready if you are," Revan explained. Heather nodded and he gestured towards the dining room. As she stepped inside, she saw the place to put your shoes, she shook off her low heels onto the black boot mat. "So how have you been? What have you been up to?"

He showed her to the dining room, as they moved through the rooms she made comments and asked a few questions. When they made it to the dining room, he pulled out the chair for her. He pushed it in for her as she sat and he went across to the other side of the small table and sat down. "I've been alright. You almost gave me a freakin' heart attack showing up in my shop today. When I saw the press conference on TV I thought that was you in the dark suit but brushed it off as a mirage," she started. Revan looked over to her and gave a sheepish smile. She started in on her dinner, a basil chicken hash and salad. "After you left and I couldn't find you, I moved here to stay with some friends. I quit my job after my talks with you. Working in the Library of Congress is nothing but a bore. I needed a change and knew that a few of my friends lived out here. I lived with them for a short time while working at a few local libraries till I decided to open up a book shop. I opened up my shop and do some photography on the side and I'm pretty happy. I also do some consulting work for libraries to help them out. Till I saw you today, I completely forgot that you said this was your home town. So, how about your explanation."

Revan put down his silverware and rested his chin in his hands as he began his story. "First of all, like I told you back then, you're smarter than me when it comes to knowledge of books. I returned to work and kept things up like I always did and continued to ask them to let me retire or anything so that I could do something else. I finally got my chance last year.

"I was chasing a serial killer from

Europe to the states. This guy was a new level of retarded. He had two goals in life, to be the world's greatest cracker and to be as infamous as "Jack the Ripper". His down fall is that once he was being tracked as a cracker, we soon found out about the killings. A rookie agent messed up a trap we set for him and he ran. He fled from Europe to the states and ended up here in Michigan. I tracked him here but needed help so I assembled a team of detectives from different cities and different fields. To our success, we caught the S.O.B. and he ended up back in Europe where he got the death penalty that was taken out immediately. You would be surprised how many countries are willing to do an immediate death penalty given the right case. But any way, I saw how well things worked with the group so I talked to the higher ups about a new investigation unit here in the states. For some reason they said yes. I figure they were ready to get rid of me any way they could. I was always in an argument with a boss about an order or I was disobeying an order because I didn't like it. Meh, now I don't have to deal with them anymore." Revan started picking around his food a bit.

Heather looked at him with a calm look that hid a feeling of great surprise at his story. "Ok, I get the story, but why Michigan, let alone Muskegon. Why chase serial killers alone. And why the heck is he a cracker," she inquired.

Revan explained, "The law enforcement community and the media don't like to distinguish between hackers and crackers. I guess because then someone may actually be innocent and they have to think of extra words when writing or talking about it, so they just put down everyone as hackers. Hackers by definition are creative problem solvers and that's all they do. But crackers use their problem solving skills to cause harm. Anyway, I chose Muskegon because its' my home town. I chase serial killers because my thought is, no matter what anyone says about that there is always four serial killers active in the United States, I feel that statistic is wrong. There are tens of thousands of people that go missing every year and most of the time; they are never heard from again. No calls, no letters, no bodies. So there could be many more serial killers out there then we could even start to think about. So this unit, if successful, will be implanted into every state in the country to go through all the missing person files, cold case files and homicides that have taken the back burner and see if a serial killer is hiding there and hunt his butt down and put em' behind bars till the building crumbles on top of em'."

After the old questions were out of the way, they both sat back and ate. They talked of old memories and such. Throwing jokes back and forth, finally settling in like the friends they once were. When dinner was done, Revan showed Heather around the rest of the house. She made the idle joke from time to time about his furniture. They stayed in the basement and had a game of 8-ball pool. Heather won and Revan bowed to her skills with the cue. As they headed up stairs, the weather turned to rain and Revan showed her his little sanctuary in the back of the house. Through a door off the hallway, a room with glass walls and ceiling.

"This was what I wanted most out of the house," he said. They walked into a short glass hallway into a hexagon shaped glass room. A custom built seat lined the room. He gestured for her to sit and he took a place across from her. The rain falling on the glass was so relaxing that Revan spread out on the seat and put up his feet. "I wanted a room to go and enjoy the weather, mostly the rain. I always loved to sit next to a window listening to the rain and thunder while reading a book. By the way, where did you get your degree? And how did you end up working at the Library of Congress. Those were things you never told me about."

"Well after I graduated high school, I applied to a bunch of colleges and universities. I applied to Yale as a joke and actually got in. I got my degree in literature after working my butt off," Heather said. "One of my professors saw how hard I worked and loved to be around books and she decided to help me after I graduated. Her sister works at the Library of Congress and got me an entry level position. I worked hard and made my way up the ranks. I put in all the hours I could and learned as much about all of the books there that I could. My research skills helped me out in getting around there. I guess it was all of that that helped me get notice my your old bosses into helping you."

Revan started, "I do need some help again. I'm sure you have seen the news about this killer I've been chasing." Heather nodded. "Well I need some help getting into this guy's head. So far we can't figure a pattern. Outside the fact that he kills everyone in the house, uses anything within reach and goes way over board to make sure the person is dead. That and he wears the same boots to each crime scene. The times in-between attacks are varied and the places always different. They are in different parts of the state and the size of the cities are different. So far he hasn't stuck to small towns or big towns. He has stabbed, beat, suffocated, and drowned his victims. He even walked up to a police officer and beat the guy with his own golf club. Just strolled on up and started hitting him. As far as the evidence suggests, this guy is working alone. He leaves behind mountains of evidence, fingerprints, blood, hair, and boot prints. Our only real problem is we don't have a name or a face to put on this psycho. I hate to say it, but so far it looks like we may only catch this guy by a total fluke of nature."

"If I know you as well as I knew you back then, I know that you will catch this guy," Heather said coolly. "I'll sit down and see what I can come up with and let you know tomorrow or the day after at the latest." Revan gave her a smile of relief. He knew that he could count on her for help. "I remember the times when we would relax at my apartment and the weather was rainy, you would grab a book and sit next to the window and let the world go. You use to walk in the rain while everyone else ran. No umbrella or rain gear, just what you had on. You never seemed to get sick from it, but you always enjoyed strolling about."

They spent the next few hours talking remembering the days that had past. Heather went home a little before 11 o-clocks. The rain had stopped. Revan walked her to her car. A bit older vehicle. A red Pontiac Sunfire, Revan guessed it to be from the mid to late 90's. No rust to be seen anywhere and the interior was immaculate. He gave her one last hug before she left. He went back inside feeling good after being reunited with his friend. He walked up the stairs to his room hoping anything she could come up with about the killer would help them in some way to catch him. He took his clothes off and slid into bed hoping that the following day would bring some more answers and not leave more questions.

Chapter 11

Revan sat down at his desk. No one had shown up to work yet. The early morning hours were not a good time for him, but sleep would not return for him once he awoke. He was rereading the files. So far nothing had occurred to him but he hoped that something would. He had heard back from Heather for a beginning report on the killer. Her research in psychology books created a list of information about the killer helped pin his mind down but other than that, nothing came out of it. The killer was believed to be uncomfortable staying in one place for a length of time, most likely because of the killings. He would know little fear in his life if any at all. Remorse would be nothing but a word to him. When he went to kill, he lived on pure rage. He would most likely not have a job and if he did, it would be something that involve travel or working at a place that would allow him to roam. He would show up to the scene wanting to kill but have no plan on how to end the lives of his victims. He may kill everyone to help keep witnesses to a minimum but with all the evidence he leaves behind it throws that part against the wall. It was maybe the fact he knew he was not in the system so he just wanted to keep his face and name away from the police.

Revan went down to the chief's office and briefed her on the report. The rest of the team had been briefed about the report the day before. The chief was unhappy about Revan using an outside source to get a profile of the killer. She shrugged it back and gave up knowing that Revan wouldn't give in and keep doing things his way. Slowly the team showed up. They had no new information from their informants that could help. Melissa was the last to show up and walked to her desk. As she sat down, her phone rang. Everyone stared at it like it was a rattle snake. The chief walked in looking at everyone. She gestured to the phone that was still ringing. Revan sat down the files and walked over to the phone. He picked it up and answered. "This is Lieutenant Revan Lygar. What going on?"

"This is Lieutenant Norths in Marquette up in the U.P.; we have another body for you." Revan hung his head. "Where in Marquette," Revan asked. "On West Magnetic Street. Just look for all the flashing lights. We know you are down state but we will be here for a long time sorting this mess out," Norths said. Revan said, “Ok, we’ll be there as soon as we can. Thanks for letting us know.” He hung up the phone with a look of dismay and agitation.

"Alright everyone. We have another name to add to the list. We have to get way the heck up into Marquette Michigan up in the U.P. It'll take about 8 hours to drive there," Revan said as he sat on the edge of Melissa’s desk.

"Take a plane, it'll cut off a lot of time," Chief Waterfurd said with everyone turning in her direction.

"When did we get a plane," Revan inquired from his perch on Melissa's desk. “And when the heck was someone gonna let me in on this little fact? It would have been nice to know.”

The chief turned to walk out while saying, "You can thank Eric for it, he’s the pilot and the feds are funding the fuel. I’ll call ahead and get things set up for you."

"Well Eric, you feel like flying way up

there with me," Revan questioned. "We'll probably end up having to stay up there for a night or two but we need to check this scene out."

His shaved head gleamed as he turned to look at Revan with his dark green eyes. "Sure, my wife has a late shift tonight and we'll probably be back in time for me to take her out to lunch tomorrow any way," Eric said. His biker style clothes creaked as he leaned back in his chair.

"O.k., you head home and get your things together, I'll head to my place and swing by to pick you up and we'll hit the airport. And everyone else, check with other police districts and the state boys to see if they've come up with anything." Revan got up from Melissa's desk and grabbed the files on the case. He pulled his leather jacket off the back of his chair as he said, "check back with your contacts to see if anyone has kicked something up. Other than that, knock off for the rest of the day and we'll see you back here tomorrow." He locked his door as he left his little office space. "Let's go Eric."

On his way to his home, Revan called Heather to let her know he would be out of town for the night. Since he ran into her again, he started to talk to her every day and was back into the way things were when they were in Maryland. After hanging up with her, he started to kick himself remembering that he still owed her a dozen roses. Strange how things tend to spring up even after 4 years he thought as he drove. He pulled into his driveway and headed inside. As he started to put a change of clothes into a backpack, he decided to check in with his contacts to see how things were going.

"Na man. I aint heard a friggin' thing about this loon ball. He is one messed up dude. I hope you put his butt behind bars for the rest of time. If I get any wind of this psycho, I'll hit you up. By the way, you looked like somewhat of a cop on the news. Later dude," Ray said hanging up. Ray was one of his old contacts in the state, a former junkie turned pro car thief with a rap sheet a mile long. The same from everyone else he could think of to call. Frustrated, he grabbed the backpack and went to his BMW.

Revan pulled into Eric's driveway. It was a nice house in Norton Shores with a well kept yard and nice tan paint job on the house. The house was one story and kept in great shape. A bay window sat off to the left of the dark oak front door. A detached garage sat to the right of the house. A small fence was propped in-between the house and the garage showing a bit of the backyard and the beginning stages of a garden. The front yard was nicely trimmed and fenced in with a short wooden fence enclosing it. A small cement path went from the side of the driveway up to the front door. He strolled up to the door and knocked.

Kay came to the door wearing her scrubs for her shift that night. The 35 year old head nurse had her hands on her hips as she stared out through the door. Revan had faint memories of her from his team's first pull together case. "You better take good care of my husband, Revan," she said standing in the door. Her brown eyes blazed as she said each word. "I like and respect you for what you do but I will kill you if anything happens to him." Revan thought, it's nice to know that my life is in the balanced if he wants to do something stupid. He felt that she really could and would do it if anything happened to her husband.

"I will take care of him like I did last time," Revan replied. "But if you have to kill me, do me a favor, please do it top-less." She raised an eyebrow and bunched up her muscles and was ready to start yelling but Revan spoke too quickly. "I'm just joking and you know that. The only person who gets to see you in any form of undress is Eric. I would never mean you any disrespect."

She blew some of her brown hair away as she said, "Okay, I'll let you off the hook this time. The next one is gonna be on you."

Revan did a little bow. "Anyways, he's the one flying the plane, not me. By the way, where the heck is he? I want to get to the airport as quick as possible so we can do the walkthrough tonight."

From the behind her he could hear Eric walking his way to the door. "I'm ready you impatient fool. I gotta go honey, I'll be back tomorrow for lunch," he said giving his wife a hug and kiss. Eric had changed into jeans and a long sleeve grey shirt. Letting her go he continued to the car with a duffle bag. He put the bag in the backseat and got in the passenger side. "Let's go. I want to quick get something to eat before we head out, I'll pay if you don't mind Arby's." Revan nodded in agreement as he backed out the driveway and down the road. "By the way, you ever talk about my wife's tits again and I'll shoot you in the face. Ok?"

Revan shrugged. His thoughts trailed off, *fun fun, two death threats in one day*. He wondered how many more he could rack up for the day.

"Good, and your right, I'm the only one who gets to see her naked. Anyway, it'll be interesting at this scene. Way the heck up in the U.P. Good to know we get to go up and meet the fudge suckers that bob over the bridge that named us trolls. Least we're not a drink away from being Canadian." They both burst out laughing.

Revan took a long detour to Arbys and ordered them each a large roast beef sandwich and a Mountain Dew. They ate and drank on the way to the airport chatting about everyday things and listening to R.E.M.'s "Losing my religion". Eric kept joking about when Revan was going to get married. Revan through back a few jokes about the fact he's cheating on his wife with fast food and also gave him crap for dressing like a biker and not riding a motorcycle. They pulled up to the airport still cracking jokes.

Revan parked his car in the designated area and they both headed to the hanger with their bags. The plane was pulled out and fueled up for them. It was a white Cessna Caravan. Revan and Eric climbed in and Eric taxied out to the runway. They got the go ahead and took off. Once in the air, Revan pulled out the files and starts pouring over them once again looking for anything could have missed. While Revan was looking at the files, Eric was informed by the tower that the Marquette police would be waiting to pick them up and set them up in a hotel.

Chapter 12

The trip up was uneventful, long and annoying but uneventful. Revan spent most of the time with his eyes closed running the scenes and photographs through his mind after he gave up on the files. All of the evidence would put the killer behind bars no matter what he said, but they needed to catch the guy first. Eric spent most of his time looking at the scenery. The plane landed at the airport. The sun was still riding high in the sky ready to descend into the darkness. A police SUV was waiting for them as they arrived. The officer who awaited them didn't look like he was more than a rookie.

"Hi. I'm officer Gates. My commander sent me to pick you up," he said extending his hand for a shake. Revan met his hand and gave him a shake. "He sends his apologies for not meeting you himself. With the murder, the street was crowded with our patrol cars and news vans. I had the easiest time getting out with his car. We'll head to the scene first so that the techs can finish their work. He said that after you're done at the scene, that we would run you over to the car rental so you can have a car till you head back." Revan nodded at this. He put his bag in the back seat along with Eric's and hopped into the passenger seat. Eric climbed into the back and they were off.

As they pulled up to the scene, Revan could see maybe five patrol cars and a few civilian vehicles. He guessed that the civilian ones were the local press. They all got out after the officer parked the SUV. He led them to the shop and inside away from the press. "This is my commander, Lieutenant Norths," he said gesturing to the man leaning against the counter. The lieutenant had a trim build on a boney frame. His brown hair showed signs of going grey in a few spots putting his age around 45. He had a heavy five-o-clock shadow on his square face. His dark blue eyes looked closely at the two new men. He put down the paper he was reading and went to shake their hands.

"You must be Lieutenant Lygar," he said. He stuck out a long boney hand. Revan took it and shook. "This is Detective Eric Bromish," Revan said pointing behind him to the waiting Eric. Norths offered his hand to Eric and they shook greeting one another. "I'm no commander, just the guy in charge while the commander is in the hospital for surgery," he said answering the unasked question.

Norths started, "well I hope you two boys aren't squeamish or anything. I had to send three of my officers outside so they wouldn't throw up in here. The body is back here." He pointed behind a curtain that smelled of strong flowers from years of hanging in the shop. He made his way towards the back room with Revan and Eric in tow. "Litia Bell, 76 and still was going strong. We had to take the body to the morgue but there's still plenty left behind." Revan raised an eye brow at the comment. He soon saw what Norths meant. A few pieces of flesh and what appeared to be brain matter were laying on the floor with number tags nearby for documentation. "The lunatic beat her face in with a candle from out on the shop floor. There are plenty of blood and fingerprints on it. She ran this shop for the last 40 some odd years. She was getting ready to sell it to her friend Pam Johnson. Pam is a part-timer officer of mine.

She was on-duty at the time of the killing."

"What was the nature of the sale," Revan queried.

"Litia had known Pam from the time she was just a child up to now," Norths explained. "Litia always saw Pam as a grandchild rather than the neighbor kid. Litia being an old hippie was always having fun and willing to talk. She opened this store after her husband died in a car accident. He always bought her candles because she loved the light they make and the scent. So after his death, Litia's Heart Candles was opened. When Pam got older and needed a job in high school, Litia was quick to give her a job. Pam still worked here when she wasn't at the station. Litia decided that it was getting time to retire from the shop, so she was going to give it to Pam. I guess the shop belongs to Pam now. She's taking it hard; to lose a best friend isn't an easy thing." Norths picked up an evidence bag that had a number of pieces of glass sitting at the bottom. Some were big, most of them small. "Glass from the candle he used to kill her with."

"Ok. May I ask why you say it's our guy? No offence meant," Eric said.

"None taken. If I was in your place, I'd ask the same question. But as you can see, it's hard not to say it's this guy. He walks in, grabs a candle off the shelf. Comes back here, begins to beat a woman in the face. He kept beating her even after she's dead. Then just stands up and walks away. No clean up, a crap load of evidence left behind, and no one saw em' enter the shop or exit." Revan nodded his head slowly agreeing with him as he saw the picture build in his head.

An officer came in the back. "Lieutenant Norths, the lab just called. It's him sir," he said. "They compared the prints on the candle with the prints that were sent up here. No dought about it. He has another name to his list." The young officer left as quick as he had entered after saluting Norths.

"Well, that confirms it, "he said letting out a breath. "It's just a shame to have to see these types of things. But if people like him didn't exist, me and you wouldn't have a job. We'll send everything down to you guys. How about we get you guys a car? And if you want to, we can head over to the morgue after you're done."

"Yeah. We should do that," Revan said. “It would be good to see the body.”

"Yeah let’s get outta here. We can hit the morgue and then go to eat, I'm hungry," Eric butted in.

Revan shook his head and responded back, "You’re always hungry. But I could was some food myself. Let's go."

Lieutenant Norths took them to a small car rental place near the airport. They picked out a red Pontiac Grand Prix. Revan paid for it out of his own pocket. Eric tried to object to it but Revan told him he gets to pick up the check for dinner. When they finally had some wheels of their own; they pulled onto the street behind Lieutenant Norths. He led them to the morgue.

It was a small brick building standing off of the hospital. A few cars in the lot said that someone was working. Norths took a spot near the entrance. Revan parked next to him and all three of them walked inside. Norths showed his badge to the receptionist. The receptionist looked as if he spent all his free time eating nothing but pizza and playing video games. Norths told him that Revan and Eric where with him as they all signed in. Norths led them down a short hall. The walls were painted a pea soup green and it smelled of cigarettes and formaldehyde. A door on one side of the hall had County Medical Examiner painted on it. Norths took them into the double doors across the hall. Inside, the back wall was covered in refrigeration units for storing the bodies. The rest of the walls were painted the same green as the hall. The brightly lit room with the examination tables gleamed with the light. One table was occupied with a body and a small fattening man working and talking to himself.

"Dr. Rose," Norths called. "It's Lieutenant Norths with Lieutenant Revan Lygar and Detective Eric Bromish of the Michigan Serial Killer Investigation Unit. We're here about Litia Billing."

The man at the table turned around at the sound of his name. He was around 5' tall standing at the beginning of a pot-belly. As he saw who was at his door, he smiled with yellow stained teeth. "Good evening Lieutenant. My, is it that time already," he said looking at the clock on the wall behind them. He walked up to them with extremely thinning white hair on his head. He shook Norths hand and introduced himself to the others. "My name is Dr. Albert Rose, the county medical examiner. It's nice to greet you. You're a heck of a lot younger than I would expect. My they sure are getting them young now-a-days," he said looking at Norths with his small round spectacles. He shook both of their hands with a small fat hand. "You guys need to get either a new name or find a way to shorten it because that's a heck of a mouth full. Anyway, you're here about Litia Billing. She's over on the table as we speak."

He led them over to the examination table he was working at. His blood splattered lab coat flowed behind him. Most of her body was covered by a white sheet. There was nothing left of her face, nothing left to identify at least. Bits and pieces of bone, teeth, and some glass were poking out of the pile of mangled and destroyed flesh. "I was working on getting what I could of the glass out of her when you came in," Rose said. "Her skull is nothing but a jigsaw puzzle. I'm putting her down for sever blunt force trauma to the head as the COD. This one is a definite closed casket funeral for her. It's a shame, I knew her. I always saw her as going out at a very old age well after I kicked the bucket. Well there's not much left to say. The killer hit her with the candle a number of times. Due to the damage, I can't say where he hit her first." He motioned and pointed around the mass of meat as he spoke. "She was probably unconscious after the first few blows. Without her fighting back, he just went to town and left her looking like an uncooked meatloaf. I'll send a copy of my report and anything I find to both the Marquette police and to you guys."

Revan thanked him for his time and they left the room so he could continue his work. The three of them signed out and headed out the door. "I can take you to a motel if you want," Norths said casually.

"Might as well, then we can go get some grub," Eric said. Revan and Eric got in the Grand Prix as Norths climbed in his SUV.

They followed him to a motel a few blocks down the road. With a car and time on their hands, Revan and Eric both agreed that a nice hot meal and rest would do them good. The motel was two story job and took up a good portion of the block it occupied. The paint job was an ugly grey with a red trim that was wearing away. The old man that ran the place checked them in. He greeted them after he recognized Revan from the press conference on TV. They each got a room.

Revan paid out of his pocket again knowing that he would be reimbursed when they got home. Their rooms were on the side of the building on the first floor. Revan walked to his room almost bumping into a garbage can on the way. Eric got a room close to the front of the building. The furnishings were sparse, a bed with an old dark blue blanket long sense beginning to fade. A small TV sat on a stand past the foot of the bed. An old end table held an ageing lamp and an old beat up bible. Revan couldn't help but to think about how if you can't find a church you like, go get a room at a motel. He threw his bag on the chair next to the TV stand. He headed back to the car wondering how many times people had moved that trash can.

Eric was waiting by the car as Revan walked up. "Norths had to get back to the station to work on his report but he told me a few good places to eat," he said.

Chapter 13

The place they chose to eat was a small Denny's style joint. It was in a small building with a cream yellow paint job with brown trim. They headed inside and were seated quickly. The inside was also a cream yellow color with brown leather booths. Old photos of the area and woodland paintings adorned the walls.

Revan ordered a Mountain Dew no ice and Eric got a Pepsi. "This is getting ugly man," Eric said spreading out in his side of the booth. "I don't like it. Anyone in the law enforcement business knows that random serial killers are the hardest to catch. And here we are, our first case lands us with one." Revan with his chin rested on his fists nodded in agreement. "His MO is all over the place. So far he has killed in basically all age groups. Race doesn't stop this guy. So far he's killed white, black, and latino. He kills in different ways. Always uses something at hand and leaves it behind when he's done. He's now been officially all over this state."

"Too true," Revan said as the waitress brought their drinks. "I'll have the cheese burger with fries," he said to the waitress' question about their dinner choice.

"I'll take the grilled chicken with a loaded baked potato," Eric said. He waited until she walked away, "Ok. Back to what we where talkin about. His time frame is as erratic as they come. He struck as soon as the next day to weeks down the line. It's really starting to bog me down. If we don't at least get a half of a description soon, we're going to be sunk."

Revan sat back and took a drink. He started, "That is true. The only thing on our side is that he will slip up sooner or later and we will see what he looks like."

"I know with going over to work with you; I did get an increase in pay. But the thought of going back to everyday homicides is starting to look appealing," Eric said with a sigh. "Least then I had a chance to understand what the heck is going on and usually got someone's name or description of them. Sure we generally didn't have this kind of evidence to get a guy with, but we knew who the heck he was. Ah to heck with it. It gives me a freakin' headache," Eric said rubbing his head with both hands.

"Well let's hope that he slips up sometime soon," Revan said unenthusiastically. "Who knows, we may get lucky and he gets hit by a car or gets into the wrong persons house. We could be really lucky and he gets busted over something simple and we have his rear in a vice. So how's things been for you?"

"You know me, my wife always jumping down my throat about eating right and taking good care of myself," he said. "Then I get to come to work and look at pictures of crime scenes and dead bodies while I read through reports. Then I get you coming over cracking jokes about my wife's tits."

"Yeah, yeah, yeah. I couldn't help myself. She threatened me and it's the only comeback that I could think of," Revan replied shifting in the seat. The waitress brought their food and a refill for both of their drinks. "Thank you mam," he said as the waitress walked away. "But I didn't mean anything by it. I have great respect for what she does every day. I couldn't work in an E.R. let alone be a head nurse in one. So you're going to have to get over it and I'll try not to say things like that again. Besides, if you did shoot me, I'd take your butt down with me." He pointed at Eric with a fry as he talked.

"Very funny," Eric retorted. "But I still think back to when I first got the call last year. I had just put another case away where a man killed his wife's lesbian lover. My chief pulled me into his office and told me that from that point on to the end of the case, I was under your command. It puzzled the heck out of me when I got to the airport in Grand Rapids."

"We all showed up one by one in the hanger," Eric started. "We greeted one another but our new commander, you, still hadn't shown up yet. None of us could figure out what was going on outside the fact we each worked in a different department and a different city. And then here comes a black SUV with lights flashing in the windshield. Here a young man jumps out of the driver side door. Grabs a box from the back seat and walks over to a table set up in the middle of the hanger. He tells us to gather around so he can explain what's going on. A serial killer that was being tracked in Europe escaped an operation to arrest him. The good news was that his name is known and we had pictures of what he looked like. That when he flew into the country, he took a flight to that airport and rented a car rigged with low-jack. The bad news is that now he knows he's being hunted and could be killing someone at that very moment and the worse news was that this young man standing before us is not here to explain for the commander.

"He is the commander, aka you. That you asked for one person from each area and to find people who stick out doing their job and to get them from different cities across the state. The guy we are to catch has two dreams in life, to be one heck of a hacker." Revan looked at him intently with a raised eyebrow. "Ok, sorry. I remember that you had an issue with anyone that called him a hacker. But back to what I was saying. He wanted to be one heck of a cracker and to be as infamous as "Jack the Ripper" with killing young ladies. One of his dreams is destroyed and now he wants to make sure that his other dream still comes true. You used each of us to reach out and find him. It took us only a few weeks to find the guy. He managed only 3 kills because he spent too much time running. We managed to get him on his way to claim another victim."

"We got lucky with that. If that old lady wasn't so freakin nosey, we may have taken months to catch him," Revan replied as he finished off his cheese burger. "Instinct and luck is what helped get him. But it did give us a chance to see what we can do to catch guys like him."

They sat there talking about that time and about the case at hand. After they finished their dinner, Revan reminded Eric that he had to get the check. He grumbled a little but he was the one who picked the most expensive meal. He paid for it and they headed for the car. Revan let Eric drive back to the hotel. Eric stopped at a small store and bought a couple of six-packs of beer. Revan called and reported into the chief about the scene. He got off the phone when Eric returned to the car.

Returning to the motel, they both went to Eric's room. Revan sat in the chair and Eric took the bed. They spent a few hours enjoying a few drinks and talking. As the beers flowed, they both opened up and talked more about their lives. As the night grew late, they both decided that they needed some sleep to head home. They reminded each other to get up early.

Revan went to his room feeling the alcohol in his head. He took a long hot shower letting the hot water pour over him. When he was done, he got into some clean boxers and climbed into bed. He lay awake with thoughts of the case running through his head. As he began to drift off, thoughts of Heather began to take over. The beautiful woman back in Muskegon. The one he let go of 4 years before hand and now was given a new chance with her. Thoughts of Melissa crept into his mind battling attention.

The morning broke with a glare. The cheap curtains that covered the window did nothing to keep the sun out in the early hours. Revan pulled the pillow over his head. He rolled over a bit still with his head hidden by the pillow; he grabbed his phone off the stand and looked at the time. It was early enough to get up but the hour still sucked. He laid back for a moment and was thinking about the trip home. He had to make sure Eric was up. He also hoped that after the drinks that he would be ok to fly. He finally crawled out of bed; he rummaged through his bag and found his clean clothes. He got dressed and packed his clothes from the day before in his bag. He strapped the bag on his back and headed to Eric's room.

Heavy beating on his door rattled him out of a sound sleep. The room half lit by the sun coming through the curtains on the window. He peaked out through the window but got blinded slightly by the sun, he saw no one at his door. The beating began again, louder and harder. Eric yelled at the door, "Who the heck is it? Don't you know it's still freaking early? If you don't knock it off right now, I'll frickin' shoot you." The knocks were as loud and heavy as they could get. He reached for his gun out of his holster on his pants hanging on the back of the chair. He cocked the old .45 and hit the safety. He opened the door as fast as he could and brought up the gun. As he looked down the barrel of the gun, he saw who it was. Revan was leaning against the door jam with a big smile on his face. "Dang it man. I almost shot you," Eric said flustered. He disengaged the hammer slowly as he put the gun away.

"Well aren't we just a ray of frickin' sunshine in the morning," Revan stated. "And here I thought that I hated mornings. If this is how you are when you're alone in a room, god I can't imagine what your wife goes through with you."

"Shut the heck up man. My wife doesn't come beating on the door like a freakin' lunatic to get me up. Least she's polite about getting me up with a kiss and hug," Eric said. He was standing there in his boxers and a tank top. Revan could see his tattoos, a dragon on his right arm and an eagle with an American flag on his left arm. He headed into the bathroom with his bag and started to get dressed.

Revan said loud enough to be heard through the door, "yeah, well, I ain't giving you a kiss. You'd be lucky if I gave you mouth to mouth. Now hurry up we gotta go drop off the car and get to the airport. Or don't you want to keep your promise to your wife?"

Eric came out of the bathroom still pulling on his shirt but otherwise dressed. "Yeah, yeah, yeah. I do want to keep my promise but I'm hungry as a bear. Can we at least stop and get something for breakfast before we get there? I'm starving for an egg mc' muffin about now," Eric said.

They turned in their keys and headed for the nearest fast food joint. Revan placed the empty beer bottles against the wall away from both of their rooms for anyone to have. Eric got two egg mc' muffins with a milk and Revan ordered two breakfast burritos and an orange juice. Eric called ahead to make sure the plane was fueled and ready when they got to the airport. They ate as they drove the short distance to the car lot and turned in the car. They walked the last few blocks to the airport still eating and enjoying the morning weather. *Clear blue skies and light breeze, today is going to be a good day* Revan thought as they approached the waiting plane.

Chapter 14

As the plane flew over the trees, Revan couldn't help but to think. The crimes were so spread out and yet so close. What had he missed? Was there something that the killer left behind that went unseen? Did any witnesses go unasked? Beyond the killer, what else did the scenes, or for that matter, the cities have in common together? The cities varied in size. The crime scenes varied in terms of size, placement and traffic. The victims were different all round. What the heck was he missing?

He began to drift off again thinking of Heather. A roust of turbulence jousted him awake. As he sat there fuming over being awoke again, he ran her thoughts of the killer through his head again; a lot of rage, intent on killing but no plan, and mobile. "That's friggin' it," he said aloud. He gestured for Eric to listen to him. "What do all the towns have in common that we haven't checked out yet? The one thing someone "mobile" would use when moving around from city to city." Eric's eyes started to widen as it hit him. "Yeah, that's it, frickin' hotels and motels man. That's the one thing we haven't checked out, in any city."

They both spent the rest of the trip thinking about the new revelation. Who knew, it was something they should have done but no one thought about it. Revan grabbed a few of the files out and a note book. He made a list of the cities where people were killed. He tried to think of surrounding towns to write down too. As the plane landed and was taxiing, Revan put his files away that he took out. They both grabbed their bags and headed to Revan's car after the plane was taken care of. They climbed in quickly and Revan sped off towards Eric's home.

"What's going on man? Shouldn't we go and talk to the team about this and get to work," Eric inquired.

"I'll handle this," Revan said. "I'm gonna drop you off at your house. Your gonna keep your promise to your wife about lunch. We can take care of this. It won't kick up anything solid for a while. The locals in each city and the state boys will have to do most of the leg work on this. So go, enjoy your lunch. I see ya at the office afterwards. Make sure you also check in with your sources."

After dropping Eric off at his house, Revan made his way home. After he parked the car and went inside he called the office. "Hey Melissa, it's Revan. Yeah the trip sucked but I'm back. Ok, ok, ok. Sounds like things went well while I was away. Listen, get a hold of everybody. Tell them that I'll be there in an hour or so and we have work to do. Ok, thanks, bye," he said into the phone.

He decided to take another shower. After that long flight in a plane, he was wanted to wash the funk off. As he showered, he thought more and more about how to handle the hotels. He got out of the shower with no newly found answers but he felt better. He dressed in fresh clothes and headed out the door. He wore a t-shirt that said "I smile because I have no idea what's going on" and blue jeans, he felt the sun beating down on him. He got into the BMW and headed out listening to MC Chris' "Dungeon Master of Ceremonies" cd.

He pulled into his parking spot; he

looked around and saw that everyone was there. He strolled into the room. Leaning against the table he said, "Look, I have a thought on where to start looking. The greatest thing in common between all of the cities other than the killer is hotels. I know we screwed up not looking at this earlier but it is what it is. So I want us to start checking hotels near each of the scenes and in the surrounding towns. Look for people that stayed there around the time of the killings. I really want any names that appear at more than one location to be look at extensively. I mean it, this could bring up something. We ain't got jack at the moment.

"If the places won't talk to you by phone, call the locals there to go and talk with them. In fact, talk to the locals any way and the state boys too. They know their towns a heck of a lot better than we do and may know a few places not on the net or in the phone book. Have them check every place they can in the area and surrounding areas. Also have your contacts looks at anyplace they can and see if they come up with anything the cops can't. I want a nice long list of people by the end of the week. If any place gives us heck, then we'll get a judge to sign an order. Let the cops know too. The chief knows a few that will give us some without too much trouble. Also, ask the cops to look for any tickets for people sleeping in their cars just in case this guy doesn't like to sleep in doors. Ok, let's get to work."

The team left the room and headed to their offices to work. Revan unlocked his office and sat at his desk and pulled up the yellow pages online. He looked up motels in Marquette. He made a call to Norths first. The phone rang a few times and then he heard someone pick up on the other end.

"Hello, this is Lieutenant Norths of the Marquette police department," Norths said. "How can I help you?"

"Yes, this is Lieutenant Lygar. I have a favor to ask of you," Revan said holding the phone on his shoulder.

"Well what the heck? I thought you guys left this morning. Did you forget something in your room or something," he inquired. "I'll see what I can do for ya."

Shifting his phone to his other hand,

Revan said, “No, nothing like that. This is a heck of a lot more important. I had a thought on the way back and we’re trying to look into it. Can you look into any hotels and motels in your area and a few of the surrounding area ones also? We’re trying to compile a list of people that have used the hotels in the crime scene areas and see if any names come together.”

Norths said while grabbing a sheet of paper, “Sure, we can do that. It’ll take us a few days but we can do it for ya. We’ll have an issue with a few of the larger hotel chains but we can get it cleared up. Is there anything else we can do for ya?”

“Yeah, could you look in your records and have the local state boys look in theirs too for any tickets to people sleeping in their car. I think that maybe this guy may not always stay in a motel and could have gotten a ticket or two for sleeping in his car. Any names for that could help us out,” Revan said.

“Sure, we’ll do that too. I hope this will help. This guy has got to be caught and put away forever. I’ll have stuff sent to you as we get it. Good luck Revan,” Norths offered. “I get the feeling that your gonna need it."

"Thanks, you too," Revan said. "I think we'll need it too. This guy is a real pain. Later man" Revan put the phone down and had called Ray to his office.

"Yeah Rev, what do ya need," Ray inquired as he walked up to Revan desk. He sat down in the chair in front of the desk. "Is there anything special you need of me?"

"Yeah, I do. You're great with auto theft. I want you to check with your old auto theft buddies and other police departments near the crime scenes. Look for any cars that were stolen in one city and left in another one of the cities. Or for any cars abandoned near any of the crime scenes," Revan stated. "This could also help us if this guy is stealing cars to get around."

Ray said, "Ok, I'll call around and see what falls out. I should have a list by the end of the week. If any cars turn up, I'll have the guy's info and prints sent out to be checked and see if it's him." Ray got up and headed to his office to make his calls.

Revan called Briggs next saying, "Hey Captain Briggs, I have a favor to ask of you." Revan explained the current case as Briggs listened patently. Briggs only asked a few questions about the latest victim and scene. After Revan finished, he explained about his idea. Briggs said that he would do all that he could to help.

Revan spent the rest of the day calling hotels in the Marquette area and his contacts. A few of the hotels gave him the privacy laws bull but he knew he would get what he wanted and they knew it too. He made a list of the trouble hotels to give to the judge. He also called his contacts and had them start checking around. The others came to his office and updated him that they were also doing the same as him and knew that it was all they could do till the list was compiled or until the guy got another victim. John informed him at the end of the day that the FBI was still pushing on the group to take over the case.

Chapter 15

The lists had been coming slowly together with only a handful of issues from hotels. They gave the list of trouble hotels to the chief to take to her judge friends. The governor had been slowly getting on board with how the group had been working. They promised to help with what they could. The chief talked to her judge friends and with a bit of help from the governor leaning on them, she got the paper work they needed to get the names. The team's contacts had also been helping pull up the information they needed. Ray had been compiling a list of stolen cars for Revan but the work has been slowed slightly by having to wait for finger print checks to come back with confirmation.

Revan woke up and felt the need to relax. He decided to go out and spend some time with a few friends and give his brain a rest. He called up Melissa to see what she was doing.

"Hello, this is Melissa," she said as she picked up the phone.

"Hey Melissa, this is Revan. I was

wondering what you are doing tonight," he inquired.

"Not very much. I was gonna head out and have lunch with my mom but that's all. Why, what did you have in mind," she asked.

"I was wondering if you would like to go out to a dinner and a movie. It would be nice to spend some time with you and thought that it would be nice. I was also wondering if you would like to have Eric and his wife Kay tag along," Revan said.

She told him back, "Yeah that would be nice. I enjoy spending time with you. I do feel that it would be great to have them along. It could be a double date. That and I think meeting Eric's wife would be nice. How does meeting at 3:30 sound to you? That way we have plenty of time to watch the movie and eat afterwards."

"Ok, yeah, that would be a great time. I'll call Eric," he said with a smile on his face. "I will pick you up at 3:30. See you then." He hung up and started dialing Eric's phone.

"Yo, what do ya need man," Eric questioned. Kay could be heard in the background singing an upbeat song.

"Hey Eric, it's Revan. Me and Melissa are going out for dinner and a movie and were wondering if you and your wife would like tag along as a double date," he asked. As he waited for the reply, he looked through the morning paper at movies and show times.

"Sure man, we would love to do that. Kay loves to go out on dates and she has the night off," Eric said. "What time and where would you like us to meet you two?"

"I gotta pick up Melissa at 3:30, so how about you meet us at the theater around 3:45 or so," Revan explained. "We'll pick a movie then and a place to eat afterwards."

"Ok, we'll see you guys there. See ya man," Eric said and hung up the phone.

With his night figured out, Revan decided that he should get some work done in his shop. He headed down to his basement and walked up to the bookshelf by his desk. He reached up to the top shelf were a lip over hung from the top of the bookshelf. He felt for the small button on the right side and pressed it. On a hidden counter weight system, the bookshelf pushed down into the ground. The opening revealed a short walkway to a vault door. The vault door hid his work shop for safety and privacy.

His work shop was room where he designed and builds new guns. Unsatisfied with most guns available to him, Revan started creating his own. The work shop had a long table that ran the length of the left wall. It was strewn with various machining equipment and random chunks of metal. Most of the metals that Revan liked to use to make his guns were steel and aluminum. The wall behind the table was covered with hanging tools and metal pieces being worked on. Under the table were containers that held various type of ammunition. A large milling machine took up the far wall. The right wall held a drawing table for design work. A table sat next to the drawing table; that table took up most of the wall leaving about a foot and a half space between the end of the table and the milling machine. The table was covered with design specs and guns that were in the process of being built. Below the table were containers with bad parts, odd pieces of metal, various spring sizes, triggers, or screws. A few filing cabinets sat under the table near the drawing table that contained his gun designs. The wall behind the table held the guns that he made successfully.

Being that his work shop once was a vault, there was no cell phone signal in the room due to the thick walls and door. In the short walkway, a phone rack with a special speaker was set up to plug in his phone while he worked.

Revan walked to the vault door and swung it open. He plugged in his phone so that he could work and still get any calls that came in. He walked into the shop and flicked on the halogen shop lights. They lit up the shop in a bright white light revealing no shadows in the room. He turned on an mp3 player that sat on the table next to his drawing table. Whitesnake's "Here I go again" started playing as he sat down at his drawing table. He shifted through the designs on the table. In the upper right hand corner, the word "Judgment" was written. He was making the gun just for the fun of it; he never intended to give it one to anyone. A number of the guns that he made were sold to friends of his in the government to be mass produced to the military and government agents. There were some of his guns that he never sold and used them for himself. A chunk of the money he made from the ones that he sold went to his retirement and various groups for charity.

"Now where the heck was I on this one," he said to himself. "Oh yeah, that stupid slide hammer. Now why the heck are you sticking?" He looked through the handful of design sets for the gun to find the one that detailed the slide hammer. Revan didn't like to follow the norm of gun design. He did what his gut told him would work. Most of it was trial and error but he tended to work out the issues. "I hope I won't have to scrap the slide hammer, I need the counter weight. I have the other counter weight but I need this to help offset the kick." Still on his chair he rolled a few feet to his left down his building table. He put the sheets that showed the slide hammer on the table and picked up what looked like a heavily cut up gun. The gun was only in the beginning stages of being built. He tended to only make the guns in stages at a time so that he could work out issues like the one he had on his hands.

He used a screwdriver to remove half of the gun's side to look at the inside. "Ok, now that you are open, what the heck is wrong with you? Where are you getting stuck," he asked himself and the gun. Holding onto the gun in his left hand, he used his right hand to move the slide around to see how it was working inside. He started letting the spring pull the slide back into its starting position. He kept pulling back the slide and letting it go as he watched closely. When he pulled the slide all the way back, he let it go and it got stuck about halfway back. "Ok, this is the issue I was having with you last time. Now what the heck is your problem?" He started rummaging around the table looking for a tool. He found what he was looking for, a small flat head screwdriver. With this tool in hand, he swung over a lamp magnifying glass to get a closer look.

"Now that I can see close up, what is the issue. There has to be a spot that you're getting stuck on somewhere in here. Nothing else is stuck, just you, you pain in the butt slide." He continued to look at the area of the slide closely; probing with the screwdriver in various places. As he worked slowly, he found where the issue was. "There you frickin' are! The hammer is hitting this little bar here," he said as he tapped a support bar that the hammer was jammed against. "Now I just have to find out why are you hitting it and find a way to stop you from doing it."

He continued to work slowly trying different way to see why and how the slide jammed-up. As he worked, AC-DC's "Highway to heck" played; allowing him to work in his thoughts with no disturbances. An hour passed for him in peace and then he picked up a sound through the music as it continued to randomly play songs. It was the sound of his phone ringing outside the shop. He put down his work and walked to the phone, he paused the music as he went by.

"Yellow, this is Revan." He asked, "What's up?" He walked out into the basement to get better reception.

"Hey, it's Heather," she said. "I was wondering if you're busy today. I was hoping that you wouldn't be. I'd like to spend some time with you today."

"Nah, I'm not really busy. I got the day off but I will be busy tonight. But other than that, I will be free till about 2:30 or so. If you want, we could go out to lunch," he said sitting at his desk.

She said, "Yeah that would be great. We can go to the Grill House. Do you remember where it's at?" As she was talking, Revan could hear her rustling through a closet. He could tell by the sound of hangers sliding across a metal pole.

"Yup, I remember alright. It's on Summit, off of Henry. I'd never forget that place, it was my favorite place to eat before I left town," he said. "I'll get ready and pick you up in an hour, that'll give us time to be there after they open and eat. So let me let you go so I can get a quick shower and get ready. I'll see ya in an hour. Later."

"I'll see you then. This is gonna be fun. See you soon. Bye," she said as she hung up the phone.

Revan put his phone in his pocket. "I guess no more work for me today. Least this will keep me busy," He said to himself as he turned off the mp3 player and the lights. He swung the vault door shut and locked it. The bookshelf was pulled back into place and he headed up stairs. He climbed in the shower and was happy that his day was at least turning out to be a good one. He hoped that the night would be good too.

Chapter 16

Revan put on a dark grey dress sweater and dark blue cargo pants with a pair of black boots. He headed out the door deciding which car to take. With the days being warm, he decided to drive in style. He climbed in and opened the garage door with the switch and pulled out to the drive way. He hit the switch again and saw the door close behind him. The car is shifted into 1st gear and the Viper turned onto the road, headed for downtown.

He pulled up to Heather's apartment building on Mitzi Street. The apartment was part of a nice neighborhood of similar buildings. The building was red brick and three stories tall. It was easily 3 apartments wide. Revan felt that the place was decently priced which showed that Heather was doing good on her own with her shop.

Heather came out of the front door quickly. She was dressed in a rust red sweater with an orange shirt underneath, a pair of black pants and black tennis shoes. She walked casually to the car seeing Revan behind the wheel. She smiled and offered a short wave as she neared the car. He could see her admiring the blue with white racing stripe paint job. She opened the passenger door and slid into the black leather seat. "Wow, nice car. I didn't know you had a car like this," she said with a smile. She pulled on her seat belt as Revan backed out of the parking space. "It's nice to see you. It's been a few days but I know you have work to do."

"Thanks, I don't like to take the Viper out too much. No need to tell everyone that I have some money," Revan said as he looked over to Heather. He pulled on to the road and started to head to Norton Shores for the restaurant. "I differently don't want to show up on the news driving this and have people accuse me of being paid a lot of money for nothing. We're already getting crap from all sides," he said as he pulled onto The Causeway. "We got it coming from the hollys and the governor. I'm already sick of their bull but there's not too much that we can do till we get lucky with this idiot. The worst crap is coming from the feds."

"Yeah, I've seen it on the news," she said as she shifted in her seat. "I don't like it.

They always want to be the first to congratulate you when you do good and condemn you if things don't go right. I have to say that I'm not surprised with how they act. They don't have to do your job," she said as he turned on Shoreline drive. "I would love to see them do your job and do any better."

Revan said with a slight laugh, "Not a chance in heck would I let that happen. Every crook in the world would be running around. Any way, they wouldn't do it; nobody would be there to kiss their butts if they had my job." He pulled on Hackley Ave and then jumped onto Henry St. "Well no matter what they say and do; the case will be solved when it gets solved. There's no way to solve a case in no time just because you want it done. If I could magically make this guy appear and convict him; I would do it. It's not like I want to drag this out. The longer he runs around, the more people die by his hands." The Viper pulled on W Summit Ave and into the Grill House parking lot. Revan found a spot and parked so he could just drive forward out. "Well let's not talk about this stuff here. I'm getting sick of this case."

Heather climbed out of the car and said, "Yeah, I don't blame you. We can talk about other things while we eat." The restaurant was designed like a drive-in restaurant from the 50s and the inside was set up the same way. Revan and Heather walked by each other as they walked inside. They got a table for two people and sat down in the classic style chairs. Revan ordered a jalapeno cheese burger with a Mellow-Yellow with no ice; Heather ordered a Diet Coke and a mushroom-cheese burger.

They talked about a few subjects as the waited for their food. She told him how her store was doing. He told her that he had recommended her store to his coworkers. She said that a few of them had shown up and bought some things. Their food arrived quickly. They both ate heartily and enjoyed more talk. As time ticked by, more people started to come in and filled up the place. A few people looked over at them but left them be. Heather told Revan about a guy that had asked her to go out sometime and that she was considering doing it. Revan wished her luck and hoped that if she did, that she would have a good time.

After lunch was finished they headed out to the Viper and climbed in. Revan pulled out onto the road to head back to downtown. "I was wondering if you could take me to my store," Heather asked happily. "I have a new assistant and they are watching the store today. I was a bit nervous asking them to work the store alone but I really wanted to have time during the day with you. Owning a store can really make it hard to do anything during the day unless you close for the day."

"Sure, no problem with that. I'm glad that you like to spend time with me," Revan said with a grin. "I'm glad you have someone that you feel you can trust to watch the store for you so that you don't have to be there all the time. I know that you take time to trust people but the people that you trust are good people." He pulled onto Seaway Drive and sped toward downtown.

"Thanks for doing this for me. I'm glad that I could get out with you but it will be nice to check up on Holly. She's a friend of mine that I stayed with when I first moved here," she said looking at the time on her phone. "She worked at a photo shop but it went bankrupt a month ago and she needed a job. She was a manager there so this job was a big step down for her but she was happy just to have a job. It was a kind of a blessing for me anyway; I really needed someone to help me. Working open to close by myself is a real pain." Revan pulled into a parking spot next to Heather's book store. "If things keep working out for me, I think I may be able hire another person so that we both won't have to always be here all day. Least for right now we can each get a day or two off."

Revan said, "Yeah, I can understand that. I have had my fair share of long days. It does feel good to get a break from the long ones. Well I hope that things work out for you. That reminds me, I need to come in here soon, I been looking for an Edger Allen Poe book and hope that I can find it here so I don't have to order it online and wait for it." Revan shifted in his seat to be a bit more comfortable to talk to her.

"Well you better get in here soon. We got a number of books of him. We may just have what you want," she said as she looked at her phone again. "Well I should let you go so that you can head out. I should really check on her anyway. A load of books will be coming in in about an hour. I know she'll like the help taking care of them." She leaned over and gave Revan a hug and said, "Thanks for lunch. Enjoy your night and have a good time."

"Thanks, I will," Revan said returning the hug. "You have a good day. I'll be in soon. Later." He let her go and she climbed out of the car. Revan watched her walk around the side of the building to the front. She walked inside and Revan put the Viper in reverse. He put in his cd for I.C.P. "The Tempest" and pulled out of the space. As he pulled out, he could see Heather inside with a blond curly hair woman. She turned and waved to him through the window. He returned the wave with a smile. He headed to get Melissa with a smile on his face.

Chapter 17

Thrown into Coldwater was how Pulse felt. The business road trip was really starting to wear on him. There he sat on another meeting being bored out of his mind. "*Why the heck did I get stuck with this job*," he thought to himself, "*I should be running it, not working for it*."

He was sitting in a small meeting room at a truck delivery company negotiating contracts. The table in front of him looked like it was barely big enough for a large family to sit at for dinner. The walls once pained white have faded and stained to an ugly yellow from years of smoking. The ceiling tiles had too turned yellow from smoke. The darkest yellow spot was directly above the seat occupied by man in front of him. He could hear the trucks moving around outside picking up or dropping off their loads as men ran around shouting orders and directions to one another.

"Well as you can see Mr. Hill, we are still offering the same terms as before plus two new trailers of your choice for only a slightly higher fee," he told to the man sitting across from him. He was a larger man in his late 50's.

His old dress shirt was barely contained in his pants with his over sized stomach. The old red tie hung down his gut like a third suspender straining to hang on to his pants. A cigarette hung from his mouth that came from the pack in his left shirt pocket. He said, “This document right here shows exactly where your money will be put over the next two years.” He gently slid a paper to the man across from him. “You know that we have maintained a long working relationship for the past 16 years and would love to continue it.”

“Ok, I like the terms so far but I got a question for you,” Mr. Hill said as he took the cigarette from his mouth and tapped it on the edge of the ash tray. “You are saying that we will get two new trailers of our choosing. Will these be brand new trailers or old trailers that where just fixed up? And how long will it take us to get these trailers if we sign a new contract with you?” He slid the paper to the man to his right to examine as he talked.

“They will be brand new. We will be able to get them to you within two weeks of letting us know what types you need,” said

Pulse. He shifted in his chair slightly to look into his briefcase more easily. He pulled out a magazine booklet and slid it to Mr. Hill. "As you can see, we are offering the full line of trailers with any available option that you may need. They will be covered under the same terms as the rest of the trailers. We will also have a new emergency repair service ready in six months. It will be a specialty team that will be available any time to come out and offer any assistance needed. They will always be in a range of about an hour to a half an hour away."

Mr. Hill looked at the booklet briefly and slid it over to the man next to him too. Dranns looked at the weasely lawyer next to Hill. His grey suit looked like he just picked it up that morning. The round eye glasses kept sliding down his large nose as he looked at the papers given to him by Hill. He looked at the papers in front of him with shaking hands. "Mr. Hill, these papers look in order to me so far," he said in a squeaky voice.

"Well I like it so far Mr. Dranns," Hill said as he sat farther back in his chair while lighting a new cigarette. "But as I look at the time, I was wondering if you have a problem taking a break for lunch." He let out a series of smoker's coughs. "I have a previously arranged lunch date with my son and this is the only time he will be available before he leaves for New York."

Pulse sat forward a little and said, "No sir, we can do that. In fact, I haven't had a chance to have breakfast yet. We can take a break and then get back together to finish up. Mr. Sampson can look over the paper work and then we can talk when we get back."

"Ok, we'll do that. We can meet up back here in let's say an hour and a half. That will give John here time to eat and read." He pointed his fat thumb at Sampson making him jump slightly. "We'll talk again then. If you're looking for a good place to eat I can suggest a few places if you like," Hill asked Pulse.

"No thank you sir. I saw a place on my way here that looked good so I'll head there. So I will see you gentlemen in an hour and a half," Pulse said as he packed his briefcase back up and stood to shake Hill's hand. As he gripped the sweaty hand he said, "Till then Mr. Hill.

Enjoy your lunch with your son sir." Pulse went out to his car in the front lot. He got in and headed for his destination. He knew that there would be no time for food where he was heading. He had felt the pulse all throughout the meeting.

Chapter 18

He pulled into the back parking lot of Terry's Bar and Grill across from the church on Vans avenue. The place looked more bar than grill with only one vehicle in the lot. Pulse knew it had to be the owner's truck. The sign on the front door clearly showed that the place was open but no one wanted to come. Pulse liked this; it would help him with his work. No need to have to deal with more people than he needed to. He reached into the back seat of his car for a backpack on the floor. He had put the bag together for times when he knew that he would need it. It contained a change of clothes in case he needed to change really quick.

He got out of his car and took the backpack with him. He walked up to the fire exit door in the back of the building. He put the pack on the ground by the door. That way he could just reach out and grab it if he needed it. He walked around to the front of the building and pushed his way through the front door.

The inside of the place did not surprise him in the least. Booths lined the wall with old cracking red leather cushions. Wooden tables and chairs were spread out randomly around the room. A full bar lined the length of the back wall with wooden stools lined up across the length of the bar. Shelves with various types of liquor line the wall behind the bar along with a few mirrors that reflected the dull atmosphere. A computer cash register sat against the wall below one of the mirrors

Behind the bar was a man in a black t-shirt. A young woman sat on a bar stool talking to the man behind the bar. They heard Pulse walk into the place. The man called to him. "You can pick any spot that you want." The man then headed to the left side of bar and walked down a hallway and appeared in the small window a minute later as the woman walked towards Pulse. He picked a booth and sat down.

"What can I get for you sir," the woman said as she walked up. She looked to be in her late 30's with long blonde dyed hair. Her brown eyes looked about him wearily but happy for a customer. She was wearing tight blue jeans and brown cowboy boots that showed off her long legs. Her large chest was shown tightly through her white t-shirt. A small black apron hung around her waist with a few pens sticking out the pockets. She pulled out a small receipt book and pen. "We've got a lot of things here," she said to him.

"I'll take a burger and fries. Can I also get a beer," he asked her with a smile.

"Sure, we can come up with that. Can I also get your ID," she inquired. Pulse looked at her with a questioning look. "We just need to hold onto it till the meal is paid for. I know it sounds odd but we do it so that people won't run out on a bill."

"I can understand that. Here you go," he said as he handed over his ID to the waitress. "If you can total up my bill when you get back, I can take care of the bill right away so that you don't have to worry." He looked at her with an understanding look as she walked away.

She walked around to the side of the bar and walked behind the bar setting his ID down behind the bar. She handed the order receipt to the man in the window who went right to work making the food. She walked over to the cash register and totaled up Pulse's bill. She wrote the total on the bill receipt and grabbed a beer from the fridge under the bar. As she grabbed the beer, she also grabbed his ID and walked back to Pulse. He took the bill and gave the money to the waitress and she gave him back his ID that he put away. He told her to keep the change.

She walked back to the bar and took care of his bill. She put the change into her tip jar. A whole $5, but it was better than making nothing for the day she thought.

Pulse sat there sipping on his beer as the dark pulse pounded away in his head. He watched the waitress clean the bar a little bit just to look busy. She glanced over to him a few time but seemed to be comforted by his demeanor as he sat there calmly drinking his beer. He continued to look about the room at the TVs. He saw that they were off but the juke box against the wall was blaring out a lousy country song.

She watched Pulse from the corner of her eye till she felt that he was ok. She judged him to be a business man from his suit. With that settling over her, she walked over to the window and talked with the man in back. She stood there with her arms sitting on the window ledge laughing from time to time. She would look over her should on an occasion to Pulse but would do it casually. Pulse could see that as he continued his look around the room. He had perfected his ability to see what people were up to without looking at them or them noticing it over the years.

He liked to watch people. To him it was a sport to watch people and see if he could guess what they were going to do next. He had gotten good at it. He was pretty good at his guesses and uses it to help him with his work. He started making guesses at what the waitress would do next.

His guess was that she would be there another minute or so and then walk away to clean the bar for a minute till the food finished cooking. He watched her closely and as he saw her, she walked away and started cleaning the bar a bit. His guess was going well so far but she changed it a little by stopping cleaning and going to the bottles on the shelves and organizing and rotating the bottles so the labels would be faced out for pouring drinks. Pulse was not surprised by this because it was a sensible thing to do for her cleaning. Little things like that came up during his guesses but he used it to help him hone his guesses to be better. The guesses also helped him in his job so that he could find a way to get what he needed done to get his contracts.

As she got about halfway down the bar shelves, the man in the kitchen put the food on the window ledge and tapped the bell on the ledge. The waitress stopped what she was doing and walked down and retrieved the plate of food. She then walked down the entire length of the bar to get around to the front and brought it over to Pulse.

He sat there and looked at the food freshly made. His mouth watered and he started eating his fries with no ketchup. When he told Hill that he hadn't had breakfast, he hadn't lied. The waitress walked away to let him eat in peace. She put her hands on the window ledge and started talking to the man cooking. Pulse watched her some more and started making more guesses as he began to eat his burger. He saw that she started bouncing a little and made his guess.

He believed that she would very soon head to the bathroom. He had noticed that many women that he watched would bounce slightly or cross their legs when they need to use the can. As he bit in more, his guess came true. She walked down the bar and headed back into the hallway. A sign over the hallway said restrooms and Pulse knew he was right. He sat his burger down and stood up from the booth as he saw her go into a bathroom.

Pulse walked into the hallway and decided that the man would be first. The dark pulse pounded loudly at him and he knew it was the right thing to do. As he entered the hallway, he saw five doors. The two on his left were labeled as the restroom. The one at the end of the hall said exit on it. The two on his right both said "Private, employees only". He walked to the back one on his right and saw that it has a small window in the door. He knew it had to be the kitchen and pushed open the door.

As he walked in, he saw a container with various utensils. He reached in and grabbed a fork and gripped it tightly in his right hand. As he did this he heard the man speak.

"Hey Wanda what are you doing back here. I told you to keep an eye on that guy," the man said. Pulse rounded the corner and saw the man standing there with a spatula in his hand. He was in his early 50's with his black hair turning grey. He was lean with a hard face and black hard eyes. His black t-shirt hung on his frame tucked into faded blue jeans. A dirty white apron hung on his waist. "What the heck are you doing back here? You're not allowed back here. Now leave before I throw your butt out onto the sidewalk with my boot up your rear end." The man shifted his weight and stepped closer to Pulse waving the spatula around lightly.

Pulse lunged at the man throwing his right hand forward at the man's face. He saw the fork imbed into the guy's face. He put all of his weight onto the guy and forced him against the still hot stove. The guy screamed as the fork lodged in his cheek and screamed yet again as his back burned on the stove.

"Get off of me moron," the man screamed as Pulse continued stabbing him. "Get out of here. Let me go." He continued thrashing and fighting back. Pulse winched as the spatula smacked his left ear making it ring.

Pulse felt the spatula hit against his head and shoulder more. He continued to stab the man. He aimed for his chest, neck and face. He felt each time as the fork penetrated the guy's skin. The more the man thrashed and fought, the more the blood was thrown about the kitchen. His grey sneakers slipped on the floor and he fell sideways down to the floor. Pulse jumped on him quickly stabbing some more. He finally got the fork to a good spot. The fork pushed right through the guy's left eye. Pulse yanked the fork back out with a sickening pop. The man let go of his spatula and put both of his hands on his eye as he screamed. With him distracted by his eye, Pulse pushed the fork into the man's neck with all of his strength.

The fork dug into the man's neck. Pulse began twisting the fork back and forth. The more he twisted the fork, the more blood flowed. The man's thrashing quickly became less and less. Pulse continued to stab at the guy. With the man finally just laying there dead, Pulse heard a noise behind him.

In the doorway stood the waitress with a look of terror on her face. "Oh my god! What the world?! No," she screamed as she turned around to run. "Oh god no!" She disappeared around the corner and Pulse heard a door slam.

Pulse was already on his feet and moving. He left the fork in the man's other eye. He walked out of the kitchen into the hallway. He stood there for a moment listening for a sound so he could locate the woman. Soon he heard a small crash and whimpering to his left. He placed his ear against the door. He assumed that it was the manager's office. He heard the whimpering again through the door. He turned to face the door and picked up his right foot. He kicked the door with all of his might. It flew open on the second kick. He saw the waitress cowering on the floor against the far wall. The phone was on the floor but he saw quickly why she wasn't using it. It was an old rotary phone and had broken open when it fell to the floor. Pulse rushed into the office to finish what he started.

Chapter 19

Revan arrived at Melissa's apartment shortly before 3:30. It was an old red brick building off McCracken Street on Harbor Drive. The apartment was two stories with window boxes hung outside the windows. He could see curtains hung in all of the windows. The main entry door looked like a white metal security door. A set of four mail boxes lined the wall near the door. Three cars were parked in the parking lot.

Revan pulled the Viper into an empty spot and looked at the cars nearby. He spotted Melissa's car at the end of the line of cars. He climbed out of his car and prepared to walk to the door. He glanced at the car one over from his spot and saw an elderly woman with groceries. He saw that she had three bags and was struggling to get them all. He decided to walk over and give her a hand.

"Excuse me mam, can I give you a hand," he asked her. She stopped and looked at him. She looked to be in her 70's with a full head of white hair. Her long light brown wool trench coat was wrapped around her loosely.

She had kind blue eyes that looked at Revan suspiciously for a moment but quickly changed to grateful. “I’m here to pick up a friend and was wondering if you would like a hand to the door?”

“Oh that would be wonderful. Thank you very much young man,” she said to him. “I’ve seen you on TV talking about that killer. It took me a moment to recognize you. Well not you but your boss but I did see you sitting there. You looked like you didn’t want to be there. I hope you get that man. He sounds like the devil’s playboy to me.”

“Yeah, I hate press conferences. The reporters always try to make cops look like idiots,” he responded. She handed him two bags and she picked up the last bag and her purse. “I hope we get this guy soon too. By the way, which apartment does Melissa live in?” They walked towards the door.

“Oh, well she’s on the second floor on the left side of the hall. Hold on a second please. Gotta unlock this door,” she told him as she began fumbling with her keys. She found the key and opened the door. “I’m here on the first floor on the right with my husband Herb." They walked to the door and she knocked lightly. A moment later an elderly gentlemen opened the door. "There you are Herb. This young man was giving me a hand. Could you please take his bags so that he can go see his friend?"

"Ok, ok. You can give me those bags young man," said Herb in a croaky voice. He too looked to be in his 70's and slightly stooped over from a slight hunchback. He was dressed in a grey sweat shirt and matching pants. White wisps of hair laid upon his head in a bad comb-over."Thank you for helping my wife."

"Yes, thank you young man. By the way, I didn't get your name," the elderly lady said.

Revan said as he handed Herb the second bag, "My name is Revan. It's not a problem, I'm always happy to help. I hate to be rude but I got to be going."

"It's no problem, thank you again young man. Have a nice day," she said as she raised her hand to wave. Revan waved back to her as she closed the door. He walked up the stairs and knocked on Melissa's door.

Melissa opened the door with a smile.

"Hi Revan. I saw you helping out Emmy with her bags. That was nice of you," she said sweetly and then gave him a hug. "It's good to see you. Did you get a hold of Eric," she inquired as she stepped out of the door and closed it behind her.

"Yeah I did. Him and his wife Kay will meet us at the theater," Revan said as they walked down the stairs. He opened the door for Melissa and went out behind her. "When we get there, we'll all figure out a movie to watch and then go out to eat." He opened up the door for her and let her climb in the car. He then walked around to his door and got in. He started up the car and pulled out of the parking spot. "They should be at the theater by the time we get there."

"Ok. It's nice to go out with friends and have fun. This case is crazy and it's nice not to have to look at the paperwork and photos of it every day," she said. Revan pulled out of the parking lot and headed towards the theater.

They pulled into the cinema parking lot and found a spot with ease. Revan and Melissa both got out of the Viper. A slight wind picked up and Revan noticed Melissa's light blue draped knit top blowing with the breeze along with her lightly curled blonde hair. She walked silently in her black tennis shoes and blue jeans. They both looked at front doors and waved at Eric and Kay standing there.

"Hey guys. How are you two doing," Kay called to them. She was wearing a grayish-purple draped top with a fashionable knot in the middle. Her hair was lightly curled like Melissa's hair. She was wearing black jeans and black low heels. "It's good to see you both."

"We're good. Revan showed me what a nice guy he can be. He helped one of my neighbors bring in her groceries," Melissa said sweetly looking at Revan. Eric walked behind Revan and slapped heavily on the back.

"Well that's good to hear man. I'm glad that you can do that stuff. You are a good guy after all," Eric says in a smug tone to tease Revan. Eric was wearing dark blue jeans and white tennis shoes. He was donning a black striped button up shirt.

"Yeah, yeah, yeah. Would you three

ladies like to head inside and see what's playing today or we can hang out here all day," Revan asked in a happy tone. He reached over and grabbed Melissa's hand and started toward the doors. Eric wrapped his arm around Kay's shoulder and followed them inside.

They looked at the list of movies and times. They talked back and forth while deciding on a movie. They finally settled on a comedy movie. Eric paid for all of their tickets. Revan bought one large popcorn for everybody and four small pops. They headed down the hall and into the theater room. Eric found them some seats in the back of the theater and they all settled in. Eric sat with his wife on his left and Melissa sitting next to her. Revan sat down next to Melissa and offered her some popcorn. They sat there for a few minutes talking until the previews started. They all quietly discussed each of the previews and said whether they would like to see the movie or not. When the movie started, they all sat back to enjoy they show. They spent the movie laughing and enjoying each other's company.

As the credits rolled for the movie, they

all walked out of the theater discussing which parts they liked the most and the one's they liked the least. "Hey, we should head to Olive Garden for dinner. It would be a nice meal for the day," Revan said to everybody. They all agreed to it and got into their cars.

Before Revan could pull out of his spot, he received a call from Barry. "Hey Barry, what do you need," asked Revan. He shifted in his seat with a feeling that he was going to get bad news.

"I have so bad news for you." Revan's heart sank. "I got a call from the state cops down by Coldwater," Barry started. "We have a few more bodies today. A concerned citizen looked in on a bar where his friend is the owner because he did not see anyone when he went inside. He found a waitress dead and called the cops. When they investigated the scene, they found a waitress dead in the owner's office and the owner dead in the kitchen. They saw the look of the place and felt it could be our guy. While they got a hold of us, they ran some prints they found. The prints are a match to our guy."

"Ok, get a hold of Derek and get down there. Take a look around and let me know what you find. You should get moving because it will take you a couple of hours to get down there," Revan told him. "Give me a call when you are done."

"You got it boss. Talk to you in probably about three to four hours. Till then man," Barry said hanging up the phone.

Revan gave Melissa a quick rundown of the phone call and she just shook her head.

Revan led them to the Olive Garden on South Harvey Street by the Lakes Mall. Both cars found a good spot to park and all four of them got out of the cars. Kay commented on the beautiful weather and they all agreed. They went inside as Revan held the door for them each to enter. Revan quickly stopped Eric on his way in and let him know about the new bodies. Eric shook his head too and walked in.

They got seated in a nice booth area. The waitress took their orders and walked away from the table to get more orders. As they waited for their food to arrive, they got into a short discussion about the case. The food arrived quickly despite the amount of people dining. They ate in a slight silence due to the new bodies. When it came time to leave, Revan paid for his and Melissa's meal and Eric took care of his and his wife's meals. Eric offered for Revan and Melissa to come over to their house for a few drinks and some time to talk and not think about the case. Melissa and Revan both agreed to go over.

Chapter 20

Both cars met at Eric's house. Revan was behind because he stopped and got gas for the Viper. During the drive, he and Melissa spent time talking about the case and the new bodies. They both expressed their desire for the case to end soon and about being together.

Revan brewed over that fact that he was torn between Heather and Melissa. He knew that he had given Heather his ok to go out with the other guy but he felt a twinge of jealousy. Due to his blessing to Heather and the fact that he was on a date with Melissa he tried to settle his mind on being with just her for the time. In the back of his mind he knew that he would continue to think of Heather and want to be with her at the same time as Melissa. It would come down to juggling time with each and risk losing them both or just pick one.

Melissa said, "I have been having a great time with you. I can't wait to do this again with you." She leaned over and kissed him lightly on the cheek. "Are you enjoying time with me?"

"Yes I have. I love spending time with you. I was hoping that we could get together next week. I would love to have you over to my house and I can make you a nice dinner," Revan said to her with a smile. "I would say later this week but with the new bodies, I get the feeling that this week is going to get interesting."

"Yeah we can do that. It would be nice to sit down to a nice home cooked meal, mainly one that I didn't make myself or get from a fast food joint. Let's hope this week won't get too crazy. This case has brought enough crazy to this year," Melissa said and she looked out the window.

Revan pulled into Eric's driveway. They both got out and headed to the door. Eric and Kay had gotten there a few minutes before hand. Eric led them into the living room. The room had a large brown sectional couch. White paint adorned the walls. A large flat screen TV sat in front of the couch with a dark brown coffee table in between. Hard wood covered the floors.

Kay sat on the longer part of the sectional looking relaxed with a rum and coke in her hand. Eric offered Revan and Melissa each a drink. They both took a rum and coke. Eric gave them their drinks and sat down with a beer. As they sat back and began talking, Revan got a call.

Revan looked at his phone and frowned. “Excuse me everybody. I gotta take this call,” Revan said standing up and walked out of the room answering the call. “Yeah Barry, what did you find?” He looked at a mirror that hung on the wall.

“I think we should go out and get lotto tickets.” Revan gave his phone a quizzical look. “I cleared the bar, you should get your butt down here like right now,” Barry said in a hushed tone. “We found something and we really want you to get down here and see it. And be quick about it, I’m not sure how long it will take till the locals start bugging us.”

Revan looked at his watch and said, “Ok. I’m with Eric. I’ll bring him with me. If I push it I can be there in an hour to an hour and a half. Keep it clear and we’ll be there soon.” Revan hung up the phone and walked back to the living room. “Eric, I hate to say it but we gotta run. Barry and Derek caught break for us at the latest scene.”

"Holy crap, really. What did they find," Eric asked standing up. "Please tell me it's good."

"Barry didn't say but he felt he had to clear the bar. I'm sorry Melissa, but I really gotta go," Revan said to Melissa in a saddened tone. He turned to Kay and asked, "Could you do me a favor and take Melissa home? Eric will be coming with me and I'll get him back here."

"Yeah I can do that for you," Kay said standing up. She turned to Eric and gave him a hug and a kiss. "Go take care of this and get your butt back here. Now go get your stuff so you can head out." Eric kissed Kay again and went to get his badge and gun.

Melissa stood up and gave Revan a hug and kissed him on the cheek. "Go on and take care of this. Me and Kay will talk for a little while and she'll drop me off. Take care and drive safe." She let him go and they both walked to the door.

Eric came to the door with his badge and gun. They all said their good-byes. Revan and Eric got into the Viper. Kay and Melissa stood at the door together and waved for a moment and went back inside. Revan backed out of the drive way. He headed down the road and stopped at a nearby parking lot. He hopped out of the Viper leaving Eric puzzled. He opened the trunk and pulled out a portable bubble police light and got back into the car. He showed it to Eric and plugged it in. Revan put the light in the Viper's roof and sped off towards I-96.

The Viper shot up to 6th gear as it hit the interstate. He quickly climbed up over 100 mph and kept on the speed. Due to the lateness of the night, there weren't many cars on the road. Revan saw one state cop on the road but he moved out of the way to let them through. They made it to Grand Rapids quickly. Revan slowed the Viper down through town and got onto US-131 and let the speed climb back up.

"Hey Eric, do me a favor. Reach up behind your seat and grab that black box," Revan said. Eric reached back and grabbed it and put it onto his lap. He opened the small plastic box and saw a black Colt 1911 with a clip-on holster and two extra magazines. Eric looked at Revan with a questioning look. "It's one of my back-up guns. I keep one hidden in all of my cars in case I need it. That one I just put in here. I haven't had a chance to put it in a safe spot. I always keep my badge with me but I'm not running all over the place with a loaded piece."

"Well, that's good to know. Remind me to ride with you on cases in case I lose my gun," Eric said. He took out the gun and put the box back where he found it. He kept the gun in his lap in the holster.

The Viper flew through Kalamazoo and got onto I-94. The world flew by as they raced by over 120 mph. The trees and farms they saw in between towns looked like a blur. Revan kept on the gas and glanced at his gas gauge. He saw that he was going to have to get some very soon. He found a gas station and stopped. He filled up and grabbed two Mountain dews and climbed back in. He sped off back onto the road and kept pushing the Viper.

"So what do you think they found? I hope this is a case breaker," Eric said quizzically. Revan turned the Viper onto I-69 with tires squealing. "I mean if they felt they had to clear the bar then they must have found something good. I am going to kick their butts if they dragged us down here for nothing."

"I got a good feeling about it but I don't want to get my hope up too high," Revan said as he took a drink. He punched the Viper harder and watched the speedometer climb higher. He saw the sign for Coldwater and steadied himself.

He came into Coldwater dropping gears to make sure he wouldn't crash. He found the street for the bar and fish-tailed onto the street. They saw two police cars sitting by the bar. One looked to be sitting in an alley and the other on the curb in front of the bar. They both still had their lights on with the officers standing around. Revan drove down the street and whipped the Viper around and pulled up behind the car on the curb.

Eric handed Revan his Colt and they both got out of the car. Revan put his gun on his right hip. He pulled out his badge from his pocket and hung it on his belt. Eric put his on his breast pocket. They walked up to the officers to see what was going on.

"Hey fellas, I'm Lieutenant Revan Lygar

of the Michigan Serial Killer Investigation Unit. What's going on here," Revan asked of them.

One officer that looked to be nothing but a rookie addressed him. "Well Lieutenant Lygar, we got ordered out by your officers," said the rookie with the other officer sitting on his car drinking coffee. "They said that they needed the scene cleared for you to get here. Our Captain got mad that you guys pulled rank on us and called your Captain and got cussed out. I have never seen him so mad but beaten." The rookie shrugged and said, "If you want the full story, you'll have to go inside and talk with your guys. We were able to shoo the reporters away about an hour ago but I think they will be back."

Revan thanked him for the information and headed inside. He hoped that there would be good news and not just some wild goose chase.

Chapter 21

Revan and Eric stepped into the bar and looked around. They couldn't see Barry or Derek anywhere. Revan looked about the room quietly and motioned to Eric to keep quiet. Revan crept silently up to the bar. He placed his hands on the bar top and looked over behind the bar. He could see Derek crouched down behind the bar looking at something. He motioned Eric to come up by him and look. Eric made his way quietly to bar and looked too. Eric made a quiet slapping motion on the bar and Revan agreed with a nod. He started to mouth "one…two…three" and they both slammed their hands on top of the bar loudly.

"Jesus Christ," Derek yelled as he jumped back and hit the wall behind him. He started to reach for his gun as he looked up and saw who it was. "Damnit you morons. I was ready to shoot you." He quit reaching and pulled himself up off the floor and brushed off his pants.

"Well it's a good thing that you were more ready to piss yourself than to pull your gun," Eric said with a laugh. Eric and Revan both shook Derek's hand. Barry poked his head from around the corner with a questioning look and Derek waved him off. Barry disappeared back around a corner. "Well what is so important that we flew down here to a cleared bar?"

"Well let me show you guys around first. It will help tell the story. Follow me over here first," Derek said walking down the length of the bar. He walked from around behind the bar towards a booth. All three of them stood by a booth table looking at a plate of food that looked less than half eaten and a beer mostly gone. "We feel that this is a meal that he ordered. Part way through eating, he got up and went for the kill."

Derek led them down a hallway to a door by the exit into a kitchen. They walked into a small room with some basic commercial cooking appliances. Shelves lined the left wall and were full of various items. The far wall had a large flat top stove, an oven and a small deep fryer. The white porcelain tile floor was smeared with blood near the stove.

"This is where the owner was found. He was stabbed with a fork of all things," Derek said as he looked at the blood stained tile. Both Eric and Revan look at the blood too. "The ME did a quick exam of his body before they took him away. He had over 40 stab wounds from the fork. They were all over his face, neck and chest. The guy even had his eyes stabbed out. They found burns on his lower back. As far as anyone has figured out about the burns, they figure that the stove was still cooling down from cooking the food when the killer attacked him.

"The waitress must have heard the attack and came in to see what was going on. She saw the attack and ran to the office. They think that she went in to barricade herself in and call 911," Derek said walking out of the kitchen. He led them out to the hallway. "By the way, they found something interesting here." He motioned to the exit door.

Revan eyed the door closely. He saw finger print dust on the door push bar and on the door jam. He asked, "What did they find? I see plenty of prints on the door but I don't see much. Give me their story."

"Well, here is the funny thing. They found his prints on there twice," Derek said as he eyed the door too. "From what it looks like, he may have used this door twice. For what, nobody knows. As far as I'm willing to give a guess, I think he started to go outside and came back in for some reason before he finally left," said Derek. He shrugged and turned to walk to the office.

Revan turned and walked behind Derek to the office. The first thing he saw walking to the doorway was the door. The door knob and the surrounding wood was all cracked and beat-up from a kick to open the door. Revan turned his gaze to the office room and started to take in all the details.

The room was small, Revan more of classified it as a large closet. A small desk was against the left wall with a small filing cabinet stuffed in next to the desk. A safe was crammed into the corner of the far wall and the right wall. A sizable panel was slightly dislodged in the far wall. A few pictures hung on the walls but that was all that adorned the white walls. A nasty blood stain was on the corner of the safe that led to the floor.

"This is the site of the waitress's death. She had a nasty ending," Barry said sitting on the corner of the desk. "She was killed violently. First she was stomped. And not just stomped, her neck was stomped. He kept stomping on her neck till it was flat. His next step is the reason for the blood on the safe. He picked her up and slammed her head into the corner on the safe. He has good aim too; he got her in the temple. From what we were told, they had to pull her off the safe to take her to the morgue. So now I guess you are wondering what we dragged you down here for."

"That is an understatement of the night Barry," Eric said from behind Revan. "You know, I was going get laid tonight. You guys just had to call and ruin it. This had better be good or I'm gonna kick your butts." Eric was standing in the door-way leaning against the door jam with his arms crossed.

"Oh you guys are going to love this. Before we show you what it is," Barry said gesturing to the room, "you guys should look around here a little. See if you can pick up on why you are here."

Revan looked around a little and let his eyes fall on the panel in the wall. "Gee, let me take a guess. Is it what's behind door number one," he asked with a sarcastic tone. "So tell me what the heck is behind that panel."

"You are going to love this one," Barry said moving over to the panel. He opened the panel with one hand. The large panel opened wide to reveal a recessed area in the wall. Sitting in the area was a computer tower. A flat panel monitor was placed next to the side of the tower and a keyboard was up on its side in front of the tower with the mouse tucked between the keyboard and the tower. A few of the wires coming out of the back disappeared into the wall.

Eric said, "Ok, so it's a computer. What the heck about it is so special? Did you find a note from the killer saying his name and that he's sorry for what he did?"

"No, nothing as fun as that. But there is something even more wonderful about it. Did you see the cords going into the wall? Follow me and we'll show what about it is so great," Barry said as he made his way out of the room.

Chapter 22

Barry led the way out of the hallway with Revan and Eric behind him. As they rounded the corner, Derek was standing behind the bar with a grin on his face. Barry let Revan and Eric go behind the bar. Revan noticed that Derek was standing in the same spot that he was in when they first came into the bar.

"Alright, so what the heck is the big deal here? Is there a genie in one of these bottles that will help us out," Revan asked getting annoyed by the mystery crap. Derek still stood there with a grin on his face and just pointed down under the top of the bar. Revan and Eric both squatted down and looked under the bar to where Derek was pointing. Revan saw something mounted under the bar and it took him a moment to register what it was. "You have got to be crapping me. What the heck is a computer web cam doing under here?"

"Follow us back to the office and I'll show you," Barry said turning around to head to the office. "You will really love this explanation." Revan followed Barry with Eric and Derek on their heels. Barry pressed the button to turn on the monitor. As the screen turned on, they all could see a program was running. "Derek, head back out there to show them what this thing is set up to do." Derek turned around and left the room. "Now just watch the screen and be amazed."

Revan and Eric watched the monitor and could see that the camera was on and looking at the area beneath it under the bar. As they watched, Derek's driver's license appeared in view of the camera. A quick still appeared on the screen and then shrunk and moved to a folder on the right side of the program. "No freakin' way. This guy is taking pictures of people licenses without them knowing," Revan said with a bit of skepticism in his voice.

Barry said, "You got that right. He was getting peoples licenses and getting pictures of them. And there's much more you will love." He pulled out a note book from a drawer in the desk that looked well used. "This is more of a journal of the day than anything else. We found in the beginning of the book that this whole thing was set up by a local kid for about $2000."

He handed the note book to Revan. As Revan started looking in the book, Eric looked over his shoulder to see. “The program is custom just for this purpose and password locked so people can’t get to photos without one.”

“Holy crap. This means that we may have this lunatic’s name and picture on the computer,” Eric said with amazement in his voice as he looked on. “I can’t believe it. Finally a freakin’ break!”

Barry continued on with his explanation of the book and computer, “The owner got tired of dealing with bar fights and other such crap that happens in these types of places. I don’t blame him for getting sick of trying to keep track of all of the idiots that cause problems. I know the whole thing is wrong and illegal but I guess it made him feel better and it helped us out. He wanted a way to know all of the morons and be able to point them out and give names when needed. He hired the kid and ended up with this.”

Revan looked up from the note book and stared at the computer. “Yeash, this is big but leaves us with a big issue. We gotta find a way past the password. I hope that our computer expert can give us some help and get in this sucker."

"Yeah, that is gonna be a big issue to deal with. The bulk of the note book just talks about people that he had trouble with and anyone that he had to give up information to the cops," Barry stated leaning against the wall.

"Ok, now we just gotta shut this thing down and get it to the office," Revan said closing the note book. He handed the book to Eric and walked up to the computer. "Barry, give me your note pad." Barry took the pad out of his breast pocket and handed it to Revan with a pen. Revan grabbed the keyboard and laid it on the lip of the computer area. "Now let's see what the heck the name of this program is before I shut it down. I want to be able to let Ron know what to look for." He hit the standard three keys on the board and brought up the task manager. He saw the program name *ID Watcher* and wrote it down in the pad. He killed the program to be ready to shut down the computer.

"What the heck is that program," Eric

nearly yelled over Revan's shoulder pointing at a minimized program at the bottom of the screen. "Click that thing Revan and see what it is."

Revan clicked the program and watched it come up full screen. As he looked at the screen, he saw that it was another camera and it was showing Eric standing behind him with Derek standing in the door way. "Holy crap. There's another camera in here and its recording. What the heck?! Eric, turn a bit till I tell you to stop." Eric began to turn to his right until Revan said, "Stop." He looked to where Eric was looking and saw that he was in the direction of the safe. He extended his hand over the safe till it came into view of the screen.

Eric moved forward and looked to where Revan's hand was and looked closer. Barry and Derek were both leaning closer with surprised looks on their faces. Eric touched the wall and could see a small black hole in the wall near the corner and above the safe. "There's a camera in the wall and it looks out over the safe," Eric said with amazement ringing in his voice and on his face. “I think that we may even have the killer killing on camera.”

“Now this is big. I can’t believe this. We need not to get too excited by this,” Revan pondered stepping back a little bit. “We gotta close this down and get it back to be looked at. I want to know what is on this computer. This just maybe the biggest break for us. I think that we all may finally get the chance to sleep well with this.” Revan closed down the second camera program and shut down the computer. He disconnected the tower and handed it to Barry.

“Let’s get out of here guys. Good job guys. You may have just saved more people’s lives and our butts,” Eric said walking out to the main bar room. He stopped at the bar with the others. “By the way, why the heck did you force this place cleared?”

“When we found the camera under the bar and then the computer in the office, we wanted to lock things down. We know that most police agencies have leaks to news media and we didn’t want that to happen here. We thought that this was a major break at the time and didn’t want it in the hands of the media and cause us more heck," Derek said.

"Well, great thinking guys. We don't need more crap from those idiots than what we already have," Revan said handing the note pad to Eric to hang on to. "You guys take the tower and head back to our office. Leave it on Melissa's desk and I'll get it to Ron. Be ready for a call from me. As soon as we know who this guy is, we have got to get scrambling to find him and put cuffs on him."

Derek and Barry walked down the hallway with the tower to head out the back door to Barry's car. Revan and Eric walked out the front door to the Viper and left with a puzzled look on the police officer's faces outside in their cars.

Chapter 23

Revan stopped at the office and put the note book and paper in a drawer of his desk. They beat Barry and Derek to the office. After putting the items away to deal with them in the morning, he walked back outside to the Viper and got in. As he left to drop Eric at home, they saw Barry pulling into the parking lot to drop off the tower. After he left Eric's house, he went home and climbed into bed and set his alarm to get up early in the morning.

Revan walked into office and stopped in one of the storage rooms. He grabbed an evidence bag and headed back to his desk. He was glad that no one was around as he walked into the room. The tower was on Melissa's desk like he asked. He left it for the moment and went into his office and up to his desk. He pulled open the drawer with the book and paper in it. He grabbed them both and set the paper on the desk. He put the book in the evidence bag and wrote the necessary information on the bag with a black marker. He put the paper in his pocket and left the book on his desk to be cataloged later.

He picked up the tower and walked out of the room and down the hallway. As he was walking out of the room, he saw Amy walking in the front door looking at him. He walked to one of the examination rooms. He found Ron Walker sitting at a desk in the back of the room.

The room had white tile flooring and the same paint job on the walls as the hallway. It was a medium size room with five office areas that lined the right wall and back wall. The office against the back wall was the largest in the room. A person sat in each of the offices. Each office had a corner desk and shelves stuffed with various papers and files. A computer and various equipment sat on the desks. The workers glided on office chairs across plastic or rubber chair mats.

Ron Walker was a heavy set man with thinning red hair on his head. His brown eyes hid behind black glasses. His face was marked and scarred with acne that persisted on returning. His fat body was covered in a white lab coat that he loved to wear. He felt that it made him look like a bit of a mad scientist and hoped it would help get him a date.

"Well I got something for you Ron and you had better be able to help me out," Revan said walking to the desk and set down the tower. "If you can't help me, I'm gonna kick your butt and get someone that can do the job." He had worked with Ron before and found him to be great at his job but annoying and lazy if he was not watched or constantly checked on.

"Nice to see you too Lieutenant," Ron said in his squeaky voice. "Tell me what you need and I'll do what I can. Just try not to rush me on it." He took the tower and looked it over and began to plug it in.

Revan said pulling out the paper, "Shut it and listen, this is very important to our investigation. On this computer are a few programs that we are interested in and files we need. The first program is called *ID Watcher*. It's a program that takes pictures of licenses with a web cam. We want a list of pictures taken with it yesterday and a time line of when they were taken and what they look like. Be careful because the program has a password set up to look at the pictures. The next is another web cam program that the owner was using as a security camera in his office to watch his safe. I want the video from yesterday. Look through it and find where you see a waitress run into the office. Let me know when you find something."

"I'll see what I can find. I'll try to find it all for you, just don't push me. This stuff takes time. I may be able to have something for you in about an hour or so. If you don't hear from me, you can come down here and see me. I'll show you what I find so far," Ron said as he turned to his quadruple monitors.

"Ok, I'll see you then. And no looking up porn," Revan said in a sarcastic tone as he walked out of the room.

Revan went back to the office to deal with the book and wait for the rest of the team to arrive. He took care of the book and the computer to make sure they were both cataloged and sat back at his desk. It took about another hour for the whole team to show up. After they all were seated, he walked up to the front of the room and explained to the whole team about the new victims and what was found at the scene. He told them all that it felt like a major break in the case and for them all to be ready to go if Ron turned up anything.

After the update with the team, he headed down the hall to the chief's office. He gave her the update and he headed down to Ron's examination room. Ron did have an update for Revan. "I got into the program for the IDs. It was easy, the security was minimal. The pictures from every day are automatically placed in a secure folder marked for that day. Only four pictures were in the file. I sent them to be printed. To help make it easier to view the pictures, I am having them printed up on photo paper to keep them nice and clear. Here is a list of the names from the licenses in the file and when they were each taken." Ron handed Revan a list of names and times in a hastily scrawled writing.

Revan said as he looked at the paper, "Ok, this is good. I hope that you found some more for us. Did you start on the web cam files for the safe?" He gave Ron a questioning look.

Ron typed on his keyboard and said, "I

was just getting to that. It should be easy. I found the name of the program he was using for it while I was looking up the ID program."

A knock at the door made Ron jump and turn from his keyboard. John said timidly as he opened up the door, "Revan, I was told you were down here. I have something to talk about. It's really important." He backed out of the door as Revan got up and walked to the door. "I just got a phone call from my bosses at the bureau. They gave me a warning to pass on but they wanted me to word it to you differently."

"Ok, so hit me with it. I wanna know what these morons want this time," Revan said in hallway with a touch of agitation in his voice. He crumpled the paper a bit in his hand as he talked.

"They wanted me to tell to tell you that they are willing to offer you any assistance that you would like from them," John said to Revan. Revan looked at him with a 'tell me what they told you' look. "They told me that if there is no arrest within two weeks, they will step in and take over the investigation. They will dismantle the group and leave you out to dry to clean up the mess. They are looking to hang this all on your neck."

"Crap, like we need their bs," Revan said pissed off. "Well I'm glad that you told me the truth. Keep this under your hat for now. I don't want the rest of the team to know yet. Once we get the information off of the computer here, we'll break the news to the team and light some fires to get this guy. You can come in here with me."

They both walked into Ron's office to see what he found. "Welcome back Lieutenant and I guess… agent. I found the video from yesterday. I was just running through it to see what I can find," Ron said as another knock came at the door. The door opened and a young woman briefly stepped in the room and handed Ron a file folder. "Thank you Mary." She nodded her head and left. "In case you don't remember from hiring her, she's mute"

"I haven't forgotten you. Let me see the photos," Revan said. Ron handed him the file and Revan sorted through the file. He took the paper with the list of names and arranged the pictures to line up with list. He quickly took out Derek's picture knowing it meant nothing. He looked at the picture that came just before Derek's. He looked at the license of Theodore Dranns. He felt his pulse quicken when the thought that this was their guy. He calmed himself till they looked at the safe video to see if it matched up.

As Ron was forwarding through the video, John pointed at the screen as he saw the waitress fly through the office door. He said, "Holy crap, here we are." They all watched the video in disgust and amazement. They saw as the waitress came into the office and closed the door. The camera only picked up video with no audio of any kind. She locked the door. As she scrambled to grab the phone, she knocked it on the ground where it broke. A moment later, they saw the door being kicked. It took two solid kicks and the door flew open. In rushed a man with medium length hair and a nice suit. He hit the waitress with his right elbow and sent her to the ground. He picked up his right leg and brought his foot down on the waitress. The waitress was out of view of the cam but they could see her hands come into view a few times.

After a few minutes of stomping, he bent down and came up with the waitress. He was holding her by her hair in his left hand. He held her up for a quick second and grabbed her head with both hands. He reared back a little and slammed the side of her head on the corner of the safe. He turned and walked calmly out of the room and headed toward the back door. They could see a moment of sun light in the hallway and it faded. After about five minutes, the sun light was back in the hallway. As it faded, they knew he was gone.

"Head back to where he came through the door," Revan said to Ron, hitting him with his elbow. "I want a good look at his face. I need to make sure he is one of these guys in the file."

Ron jumped back in the video to the point where the killer came into the room. He froze the frame and printed out a copy. They all looked at the print from the video and the photo line-up of licenses. They all stared at the video photo and the license of Dranns.

Chapter 24

Revan and John both ran into the office with the papers in hand. “Holy crap and drop the phone Melissa. Call everyone in here now.” She made the calls quickly. The team rushed into the room. Revan held up the photos as the team sat at the table. “We have a positive ID on our perp. We are looking for a Theodore Dranns. He has a Tennessee driver’s license. We got a copy of it here,” Revan said throwing the photos on the table. “John, I want you to look around a little with the FBI and see if you can find out if he still lives there, if he does, find out where he works there. Try to keep this calm if you can. I don’t wanna have to deal with your bosses or risk having him tipped off.”

“Ok, I’ll get on it. I’ll try to keep it quiet,” John said leaving for his office. He pulled out a black address book as he headed out the door.

Revan point to Ray and said,” Ray, I want you to look around and see if you can find a car with this guy. I want to know if it’s stolen, rental or what. Barry, see if you can track down any place this guy might be staying. Amy, I want you to go back and look over the list of name from hotels with Mary and see if you can find his name in any place. I want to know where he has been. A message to everyone, talk to your sources and see if you can dig any news on this guy. Let me know if you guys dig up anything." Revan walked to his desk and made some calls to a few of his contacts.

After a few hours past, no one turned up anything. Revan placed a call to Captain Briggs. "Hey Briggs, how are things for you? Did you ever hear anything about the possible in Pellston?" Revan drummed his pen on his desk. He was ready to hear some news one way or the other.

"Well things are going good here. Not too many cases to deal with around here. We are getting some flack here and there from the people wanting the case to be solved. I did hear from Pellston though. I was actually going to give you a call today. It took them some time but they did manage to dig up an old cold case," Briggs said. Revan could hear papers moving around.

"Ok, I have got to hear this," Revan said

getting interested.

Briggs started the story, “They dug up a file from about 7 years ago. One Madalin Fox, age 86, was killed in her home. She was stabbed over 30 times in the chest. Here is the interesting part; she was stabbed with a garden trowel. They found some prints in the house. They compared them to some prints of your killer and found a match. They were the only prints found at the scene that didn’t belong to the victim and they were on the handle of the trowel.”

“Wow that is a big thing. So now we know he was here 7 years ago,” Revan said jotting down the new information. “Well I have some better news for you. We have a name and pic of our killer. We got his driver’s license even.” He heard Briggs drop the phone and scramble to pick it up. “We’re tracking him down as we speak. As soon as we have a location on him we’ll give you a call to join us on the bust.”

Briggs said excitedly, “You had better call me. I want to be there to help kick his butt. He is gonna pay for every life he took.”

"I'll get back to you then Briggs. Take care and try not to salivate to death. Later," Revan said and then hung up. Revan left his desk to let the rest of the team know about the new victim.

About an hour and a half went by with everyone making calls and checking information. Melissa informed Revan that Chief Waterfurd wanted to talk with him in her office. He left the room and headed to her office. In the hallway he saw everybody running around more than ever. He knew that the news about an ID had spread fast.

When he arrived at the Chief's office and walked past the stunned secretary into the main office area. He sat down in the chair across from the Chief. "So what is it that you want? We're a bit busy right now," Revan said.

"So you have a name and picture of our killer and you fricking tell everybody about it," Waterfurd nearly yelled. "You run around with this kind of information and don't even bother to tell me about it. This is too big for you to keep secret."

Revan retorted, "Well excuse me if I'm trying to do my job. I'm trying to track this guy down and put his butt behind bars. I'm sorry I can't tell you every fricking thing every fricking second. Now if you'll excuse me, I have work to do."

"You're not going anywhere right now," she said pointing a finger at him. "I don't expect you to tell me everything all the time but a major development like this I need to know."

"Ok, I'm sorry I didn't tell you right away but it is information that needed to be jumped on." He ran his fingers through his hair. "I also don't want the media to get a hold of this before I can get him. I don't want the hollys to get his name and picture up and scare him into hiding before we get him. I don't want him plastered all over the place. It'll just make everybody's lives harder," Revan said turning to leave again.

"Alright, just don't let it happen again. I'll make sure I get around and remind everyone about their contract and not to talk to the media," she said standing up herself. "I'll make sure they know about their possible 30 years in jail and $500,000 fine for telling the media any unauthorized information."

When Revan got back to the office, John ran up to him with information. He started, "I had a buddy down in Tennessee check around for me. He found that the guy is still a resident of Madison. He works for Road Trails Trailers. He looked up the company and found that they do repairs to trailers for shipping companies across the country. They have licensed repairmen all over to do regular and emergency repairs and maintenance for shipping trailers. They hold contracts with over 70 shipping companies. Here's the kicker; Dranns's mother is the current CEO of the company."

"That is great information," Revan said with a smile. "Please tell me you have a number to this place? I need to talk to them right away."

"Yup. He gave me a number to call." His face beamed as he talked. "He said that it should get us a hold of his boss. He didn't tell me if it would be his mom or not so it makes me nervous," John said handing him a piece of paper with a number on it.

Revan thanked John and went to his desk. He picked up the phone and started to dial the number. The line rang three times and someone picked up on the other end.

Chapter 25

He checked into a new hotel later that night. It was a small run down place near Flint on West Bristol Road near South Linden Road. The room looked like the last place that he stayed in. Another crappy place to stay in but it helped him to stay out of the way. His mother wondered why he stayed in those types of places when the money was given back to him at the end of the two weeks of pay because he refused to take a company credit card. All he could tell her was that they were the easiest places to get into if he had to change route and go to a new town on short notice.

He had felt good sense the latest killings. He had worried that the waitress may get away by running out the back door but she made her mistake. She decided to run into the office and hide there. She thought that the door would keep him out; not a chance in heck. He may be getting up there in the years but he had kept in good shape. Running around getting people to kill was a great form of exercise. That and going from place to place walking around those different shipping companies helped out.

He made it to Flint early before his next contract meeting. He had about two days till the meeting and hoped to get in a kill before the meeting. He stopped at a thrift store going through Lansing. He got a new pair of jeans and a sweat shirt.

After he had finished with the waitress, he had gone to the backdoor and opened it. He retrieved the backpack that he left by the door. He took it into the men's room and changed his clothes. He got blood on his suit and had to dispose of them later. He got into the suit that was in the pack. After changing, he placed the bloody suit in the pack and walked out the backdoor. He left and grabbed a quick meal at a nearby restaurant. He got back to the shipping company in time for the rest of the meeting. He told the owner of the company that he had changed because a waitress had spilled a drink on him when she tripped. The guy bought the story and he finished the meeting. After he was done, he headed to Flint but stopped in Marshall. While there, he found a dumpster behind a closed business and threw in the suit.

He lit a match and threw that in on top of suit and closed the lid. He figured that the match would quickly set the suit on fire and be rid of it for him.

"I think this will be a great place to do my work. I think that I will get in a great kill if I'm lucky," Pulse muttered to himself. "I saw a few places that would be great. I just hope that the pulse will kick in. I am the Pulse and not a soul will stand in my way when I want them dead."

His cell phone began to ring. He looked at the screen and could see that it was his mother. He flipped open the phone and answered the call.

"Hello Theo, this is mom. How are you doing? Did the meeting go well yesterday," she asked in a rough voice from her tracheotomy. She was always calling and bugging him. Pulse hated it and hoped that she would die or just retire and leave him alone.

"Hi mom. Yes it did. He signed up again," Pulse said. "He loved the add on for the new trailers. You could nearly see him explode at the thought of new trailers." He sat down on the bed to talk more comfortably. "He called a halt to the meeting about halfway through. He had to make a lunch with his son for about an hour and a half. When he came back, he was ready to sign. He put his name on the line and said that he was glad to continue business."

She said, "I'm not surprised. That old fart loves to try tricks to get us to sweat. He thinks that it will get us to give him a better deal even though he knows that he will take it anyway." She pulled the phone away to cough. "I'm glad that you saw through his bull. The guy before you bought it and cost us $2000 in fees. That's a big reason that he's not working for us anymore."

"Well it was an easy thing to see. The old fart said lets break for lunch so the contract could be looked over. It's a stupid thing to do but he knows that it worked before so he'll keep on trying. At least we won't have to worry about him for a while, I locked him into the 5 year contract," he told her.

"Good job honey. Just a few more places

to talk to and get on board and you can come on home," she said with a cough. "I see that you just got 3 more places and you'll be home in about 2 weeks. I'm proud of you. I'll talk to you after this next meeting. Good luck honey."

He said to her, "Thanks mom. I'll see you soon. Love you and talk to you later." He hung up the phone. He was glad that she was happy and proud of him. Both were things that came to her rarely in the recent years. The only thing that bothered him was that she would never tell him that she loved him. She had stopped saying it to him when he was in college. It broke his heart then but at that time in his life it just bothered him.

He decided to go out and get a bite to eat and wonder around town. He drove around town, just wondering for a few hours and decided that the pulse would not start. He picked up a pizza and a 6-pack of beer. He went back to the hotel room and watched TV for the rest of the night. He drank the beer and ate the pizza slice by slice. After his meal, he laid in bed and went to sleep. Just two more days till the meeting.

He awoke the next day feeling good. No hangover and not feeling too full from his meal. He went out and found a small restaurant in the area. He ate breakfast and headed back to the hotel. After about sitting around for an hour, his phone rang. He looked at it and didn't entirely recognize the number. He wondered what they wanted. It felt weird for him but he opened the phone and answered.

"Hello?"

Chapter 26

"This is Lieutenant Revan Lygar of the Michigan Serial Killer Investigation Unit," he said. "I need to talk to you about some crimes that have happened across the state of Michigan."

A rough lady's voice came across the line, "Yes, my name is Margret Dranns. I am acting CEO of Road Trails Trailers. How may I help you Lieutenant?"

"Do you have a Theodore Dranns working for you," he asked her. He already knew what the answer was but wanted to go through the motions. He knew that the tactic would help get her to loosen up and talk with him.

"Why yes I do. He is my son. He is a contract negotiator for us," she told him. "We send him around to talk to companies to negotiate new and returning contracts." She pulled the phone away and let out a few terrible coughs. "Has something happened to my son? Is that why you are calling?"

He started, "No mam, nothing like that.

We have found no evidence that he is hurt. I am calling for another reason. I know this will be hard to hear but your son is a suspect in a number of murders here." He heard her set the phone down for a moment.

"Are, are, are you sure that it is him. Can you be absolutely sure that it is him," she asked with absolute shock in her voice. He could also hear what sounded like tears in her voice. "How could he be a murderer? He wouldn't do anything like that."

"Well mam, to tell the truth; he is the only suspect. We have him on video committing one of the murders. We have his driver's license photographed at one of the crime scenes. The main reason why we are calling is that we need to find him. He needs to be arrested before he hurts someone else. We don't feel that he can help himself. He will continue until he is caught," he told her.

"Alright Lieutenant, if you are 100% sure that it is my son, I will do what I can to help you find him. If you will give me a moment to look at his paper work, I will find where he is staying," she said with a cough and a sniff.

He felt no issue with her alerting her son to the investigation. "Thank you mam. This will be a major help to us. I know that this must be hard for you to do," he said to her in a calm soothing way. "I won't pretend to know how you feel or what this is doing to you. The only thing I know is that your son is dangerous and needs to be stopped. He needs help."

He could hear her take the phone away from her ear and call to someone. He heard only a muffled talk from the other end. He could tell that she had her hand on the phone. The phone became clear again and he said, "Mam, are you there?"

"Yes I am young man. I was asking for my son's paper work. We keep track of cities and hotels that he stays in. He reports the hotel he is in and lets us know how much it cost when he checks out. We reimburse him every two weeks for what it cost him plus his pay," she told him.

She coughed again and pulled away the phone again. He heard her thank someone and set papers down on the desk. "Ok, it looks like he has a meeting in two days in Flint. It says that he checked in with us about 8:00 pm last night. He had a meeting in Coldwater yesterday."

"Thank you very much mam. This is a great help to our investigation. When he checked in, did he say where he was staying," he asked her getting excited but maintaining a calm voice. He had a pen in his hand and wrote down *Flint*. He held the pen in his hand waiting for the name of the hotel.

She told him, "Yes he did. It's called the Side Road Motel. I'm not sure where it's located in Flint."

He wrote down the name of motel down and circled it. "Ok, there is one other thing you can do for me please. You said that he has a meeting in two days. Could you call him and tell him that the meeting was cancelled," he explained to her. "We need him to stay in that motel so that we can get a proper ID on him. Tell him to stay in there that you have a few other places nearby that you are going to try and set him up with a meeting. Try to get him to stay in or near the motel. Tell him that he could get a call anytime to go straight to a meeting."

"I will do that for you Lieutenant. If what you are telling me is true, I will do all that I can to help you. I will tell you this, if my son is innocent you will be the one to pay for anything that happens to him," she growled into the phone. Revan understood that she was being protective of her son.

"I understand mam. We will do all in our power to ensure that he is apprehended without incident. I assure you that we are correct about this. We will get him the help that he needs," he told Ms. Dranns. "Thank you again for your help. Good bye Ms. Dranns." He heard her hang up the phone without saying a word. As he put his phone down; he had the feeling that her tears, surprise, and even the anger were all fake; as if she had been waiting for the call all along. He put the feeling aside to deal with after the case was done.

Melissa called the team into the room while he was on the phone. He stood up and walked to the front of the room to address the whole team. "Ok everyone, I need you to listen up. I talked with our perp's mother. She confirmed that he is still in the state. He is in Flint at a motel called the Side Road Motel. We need to get ourselves over there and make a confirmation on his ID. Did anybody else get anything," he asked the team.

Amy said, "We found the perp's name on our list. He was found to be staying at three motels near the crime scenes. All of the motels he stayed at are run down fly by night motels. Just the type of places that want cash up front and a name."

"I talked around to some sources and did some extra talking around. I found that there is a rental car registered under our perp's name. It's from a Hertz in Detroit from the airport. It was rented out for about two and a half months," Ray said to all. "The car is a black 01' Toyota Camry. I got the license plate number for the car. Outside of that I got nothing." He sat back in his chair when he finished talking.

No one had anything else to add to the information. Revan handed Melissa the picture of the killer's license. He gave her the paper with the city name and hotel name. He had Ray give her the information on the vehicle.

"Ok, please take this and make up a flier with his picture, name, hotel and city name, the car make and model and the license plate number. Make up about ten fliers. Please bring them back as soon as possible," he asked her.

"Alright, I'll be right back with this right away," she said taking the papers. She walked to her desk to begin work.

He went to his desk and asked Eric to look up the location of the motel. While Eric went to look up the information; he pulled out his cell phone and placed a call to Captain Briggs.

"Hey Briggs, get your craptogether," Revan said. "We got a location on the perp. I talked with the guy's boss who also happens to be his mom." Revan could tell that Briggs was rolling his eyes at that. "She told me where he's staying at right now."

Briggs dropped the phone and sounded like he was choking on something to drink. He coughed out, "You had better not be screwing around with me. I'm getting too old to be excited like this."

"I'm not kidding with you. We are getting an exact location on the motel right now. It'll take us about three hours to get there. I want this guy in cuffs before dark. We're gonna be hauling butt there so hopefully we'll be able to cut an hour or so off," Revan said as Melissa walked out of the room to make copies of her fliers.

"Look, I'm friends with the chief at the Flint police department. I can give him a call and get us some help," Briggs offered. "I think he can help us get this guy, he's gonna have to book this guy in a cell for a day or two anyway."

"Yeah, that would be a good idea. We're gonna be in plain clothes. I want you in plain clothes too and if he'll send anybody, make sure they are too. I'll take about four or five people," Revan explained. Eric walked up to Revan and gave him a paper with the address of the motel. Revan told Briggs the address.

Briggs started, "I know that area; let's meet at Genesee Valley Center. They have a big parking lot. It's only a few blocks away. If we meet in the north east parking lot, the guy will never know we are around."

"Ok, that sounds like a good location to meet at," Revan said as he saw Melissa came back in with a stack of papers. She waved them at him a little and set them on his desk. He mouthed thank you to her and she smiled back. "Tell the Flint guys to meet us there too. No sirens and no uniforms. I'll see you there." Revan hung up the phone and checked his guns in his shoulder holsters.

Chapter 27

Revan got into his BMW with Eric, Barry and John. Amy, Mary, Derek, and Ray got into Mary's 2006 Ford Focus. Flint was Barry's town before he was hired by Revan. Revan knew the way to Flint and would rely on Barry when they got close to the city. Both cars put on their lights heading down I-96 to Grand Rapids. They passed the outer area of Grand Rapids still on 96. A few patrol cars looked to join them but broke off as they left the city limits. As they neared Lansing, they got on I-69. They both stopped at a gas station on the edge of Lansing and gassed up. Revan double checked with everyone to make sure that they were armed. They confirmed that they were. They got back on 69 and sped toward Flint.

As they neared Flint, Barry had them take the Miller road exit. Barry informed them that they were near the motel so they turned off their lights and kept their speed down. They took Miller road to south Linden road. They turned in to the Genesee Valley Center parking lot and headed to the north east lot.

They found Captain Briggs in an empty

area of the lot. He was standing next to an unmarked dark blue Crown Victoria. Two more cars were parked next to his car. Four guys got out of the cars, two from a dark brown Ford Torus and two from a black Toyota Camry. All four looked like plain everyday guys. Revan knew right off the bat that they must all be narcotics officers.

Barry recognized all four of them and went up and shook hands with them all. Revan shook hands with Briggs and saw that he was dressed in a pair of blue jeans and an olive green t-shirt under a jean jacket. He also had a black base ball cap on his head. Revan could see a gun in a shoulder holster.

Revan greeted the four plain clothes detectives and handed them each a flier. He passed around fliers and made sure that everyone was looking at them. He told them all about how dangerous the killer was and to watch him closely. The narcotic guys memorized the information about the car and folded up the paper. They folded the paper to leave Dranns face in a square. The Narc guys gave out six radios to everyone with a secure channel pad and ear pieces.

"So what is your plan Revan? I hope you got something good in mind," said Briggs. "I want to nail this guy. He can't get away."

Revan started explaining, "Here is my plan, Mary, you and one of the Narc guys take a car and go into the hotel manager's office. Act as a couple on vacation. Keep an eye out for our perp and make sure that he is not in the office. Talk to the manager and get him to tell you what room he is in and get a room as close as you can to him. Give him the money for the room to keep him quiet. I want four people to go to the building nearby and go around the back and get behind the motel. If there are windows, keep low and quiet, I don't want him knowing you are there."

Revan looked to another Narc detective and said, "Four of us will be across the street. We will look for the perp's car. When we feel we have the car there, you and two others will walk into the motels parking lot and check the tag and make sure it is the right one. Head to our rented room and wait with the others."

He stepped back to address the whole group. “I want an exact ID on the guy and I want to get him in his room. When we have an ID and he is in his room, I want two guys to stay in the back and watch his window if there is one. If there is not one or it’s beyond too small for him to squeeze through, go with the rest. Those that go around front I want to come around the side of his room opposite the side of our room. Mary and your group to come up to your side of his room. My group will come up directly to his door.”

One of the Narc guys walked to his car and grabbed a pair of binoculars and handed them to Revan. All four of the guys looked at him with a look of agreement. The rest of the team looked like they agreed with the plan too.

“Just remember, when this goes down, I want him alive. Be careful and don’t fire any unnecessary shots,” Revan said with a stern voice.

Revan, Briggs, John and a Narc guy got in the BMW and headed to their location. Mary and a Narc guy named Harris headed to the motel in Mary's car. Harris had said that he knew the owner and could get their answers. The hotel had been used many times as a secure location for drug busts. Amy, Eric, Barry and Ray headed around to the back of the motel. The other two Narc guys and Derek took a car to a place a block away from the motel to do the walk up. Each group had a radio for quick communication.

The motel was a crappy run down place. It had just one floor of rooms that went up to 20. There were 10 rooms on the left side of the office and 10 on the right. The white paint job was dirty and peeling. The red neon lights that worked were faded to an ugly pink. The sign for the motel looked like it would not light up even if it was struck by lightning. The doors for the rooms were painted red and were beat up and fading. The manager's office looked small and cramped. All of the windows had dirty blinds and had air conditioners in bad need for repairs. Revan felt that it was a place that you took a hooker or your mistress to.

Mary and Harris went into the manager's

office. They talked with the manager for about 15 minutes. They left the office and went down the left side of the motel and went into room 4. When Mary reached her room, she radioed in to the team. "We are in room 4 on the south end of the building. The perp is staying in room 2. That is the second room from the left end of the building."

"Ok, rear team move along to the south end of the motel," Revan said into his radio. "Report in on windows in the rear of the building."

Barry came across the radio a minute later, "That is a negative on rear windows. The area back here is littered with trash so we will be moving to the end of the building to avoid noise."

Revan reported on the radio, "Alright, there are five cars in the lot excluding Mary's. There are three cars located to the north end of the lot. None are black. Mary's car is located in front of the office. To the south end of the lot are two. One white SUV on the end of the building and one blue truck parked next to the SUV. Walk team hold your position till the perp arrives."

After they all were holding their positions for a half hour, a black car pulled into the parking lot. It drove to the south end of the lot and backed into the space in front of room 3.

Chapter 28

"Alright everyone, hold your positions," Revan crackled on the radio. "We have a black vehicle that pulled into the lot. It backed into the space in front of room 3. We are unable to see the plate at this time. A white male has stepped out of the vehicle. Unable to positively identify. He is wearing a blue base ball cap, dark sun glasses, a black long sleeve shirt, blue jeans and white tennis shoes."

As the man got out of the car, he took a cautious look around. He grabbed a shopping bag from the back seat and walked behind the car. He walked up to room 2. He looked around cautiously again and went inside.

"Walking unit, get your butts down here. Walk fast you guys. The guy went into room 2. Still unable to identify," Revan said to the team. After a moment of thought, he got back on the radio. "Derek, give me one of your Narc guys."

"This is Jones, Lieutenant. What do you need me to do," the guy said with a deep voice.

"We need a beer or something," Revan said back. "I know you guys are good at acting when undercover. After the tag check, I want you to go up to the perp's door and knock. When he answers, act drunk and give a bull talk to him. Tell him you're looking for someone and when he tells you that they're not there, walk away. Make sure that when he opens the door that you stumble backwards so that he can't drag you into the room."

"This is Mary. If you stop at my car, hit the button for the trunk and open it. There is a case of beer in there for my husband. You can use one or two if you need. You'll just owe my husband a few beers Revan," she told them.

Revan said, "I'll by him a whole new case if this works. Jones, stop at the car and get a beer. Take one swallow and dump some on the front of your clothes. Make sure that you keep up the stumble and drunk walk all the way to his door. Put Derek on please."

"You got 'im man," Derek came through.

"When you guys get to room 4, get down like you are tying your shoe. That will give you time to check the tag. Give us a thumbs up if the tag matches," Revan explained. "Tell Jones to do the same if the ID is positive."

Revan's group watched as Derek and his two Narc guys came across the street. As they came into the parking lot, one of the narc guys slowed from the group. Revan guessed that he was Jones. He stopped at Mary's car and opened the driver's side door. It took him a moment of searching and then he got out of car and went to the trunk. He opened the trunk and came out with a beer bottle. He opened it and took a big swig. He then poured what looked like about half the bottle on the front of his shirt and jacket.

Derek and his guy got up to Mary's room and walked an extra foot. Derek got down on one foot and pretended to tie his shoe. After a moment, he got up and went to Mary's door. Revan watched with the binoculars and could see that Derek made a thumbs up gesture. Revan waited till they both went into the room before he reported to the team.

As Derek got in the room, Jones passed by in a drunken shamble. He was doing the walk like a pro. He got to room 2 and knocked on the door. He kept knocking on the door. Revan could see that he was saying something. He kept talking to the door. After a moment, the door flew open and a man with medium length hair stood in the door way. Jones made a large stagger back and hit the truck that was parked in front of the room. He could see that the guy was talking to Jones and looked a bit mad. Revan looked closely at him. He was sure it was the guy but he wanted the ID from Jones. The guy shook his head and slammed the door on Jones. He got off the truck and shambled down to Mary's room. As he stood there ready to go inside, he gave a thumbs up behind his back.

"Alright, everyone get your selves together. We have a positive ID on the car and on our perp," Revan nearly yelled into the radio. "Back team and room team, move up to your positions by his room. I want guns drawn and ready. Make sure you stay away from his window."

Revan had the car on and in gear. He pulled onto the road and went right across to the motel parking lot. He pulled up to the spot in front of room 4. Both teams had already got in their positions when Revan pulled up. All four of them got out of the car and went up by Mary's team.

Derek told Revan in a hushed tone, "Reaves here told us that the Flint police have a few cruisers that are standing by one block down to give us assistance. They are also going to transport this guy to the local jail. They also have an ambulance standing by just in case."

"That's good. I want him behind bars right away," Revan said in a hushed voice. He quickly moved up to the door. He drew one of his Colt 1911s from his shoulder holster.

He knocked on the door with confidence. He knew that with everyone behind him, this guy was not going to get in the way. "Theodore Dranns! This is Lieutenant Revan Lygar of the Michigan Serial Killer Investigation Unit. You are under arrest for 11 murders. Come out with your hands up or we will kick this door in and drag you out."

There was no answer from inside. He looked to the back team with a look that said 'are you sure he can't get out through the back'. They all shook their heads no and he nodded ok back.

"Come out right now Dranns or we are coming in," Revan shouted. There was still no answer from inside the room. "That's it. To heck with this nice crap. We're going in," he said to his team.

He stood up and gave the door a good solid kick. The door gave a little on the kick and Revan knew it was gonna take a kick or two more to open it. Revan stepped to one side as Derek moved his way front. He picked his right foot up and gave the door a giant kick. The door flung open and Revan rushed through the door.

The door bounced off the wall and hit Revan in the shoulder as he headed inside. He could tell that his team was behind him the whole way.

As he made his way past the bed to the bathroom, Dranns rushed out of the bathroom. He had an electric shaver in his hand. The shaver was held over his head showing that he wanted to take someone out. As he neared Revan, a shot rang out.

Revan was bringing up his gun as he saw a bullet shoot through Dranns's arm and heard the thunder of a gun. The roar from the muzzle of the Rhino .357 revolver was deafening in the small room. Revan caught a glance of the Narc guy that was in his car with his gun in his hands. The barrel of the black revolver left a trail of smoke that drifted toward the ceiling.

As the bullet passed into his arm, Dranns dropped the electric shaver and stumbled backwards. He fell to the ground grabbing his right arm and yelling. Blood poured out of the wound through his fingers. The ears of everyone in the room continued to ring from the shot and it slowly switched over to a ringing of the yelling.

Revan continued forward with his gun pointed at Dranns. He pushed his gun into Dranns's face and grabbed his left hand. He yanked it away to look at the wound in his arm. He yelled for Reaves to call the squad cars and the ambulance. Barry grabbed the pillows on the bed and yanked off the pillow cases. He threw both of them to Revan. Briggs and a few others came up and trained their guns on Dranns.

Revan put his gun away and grabbed the pillow cases. He folded one into a long band and wrapped it around Dranns's arm. Amy reached down and held it while Revan took the other pillow case and tied it around Dranns's arm tightly.

After about 15 minutes, both police vehicles and the ambulance arrived. Dranns got a light patch up on his arm and was put into the ambulance. Harris road with the ambulance with his gun out to make sure the Dranns would not hurt anyone. Briggs gave Revan and his team all hugs and handshakes. He thanked them all and the Narc cops. He got a ride to the mall to get his car and head home. The other three Narc guys shook hands and went their own way to file their reports. The local police said they would process the scene and forward evidence to the MSKIU labs. Revan thanked them for the help.

His team hung around for about another hour or so. They looked around the scene and answered questions. The Narc guy that fired the gun stopped by the scene. He told Revan that his name was Perry. Revan thanked him for only firing one shot when most would have kept shooting. He apologized for taking the shot but he didn't want the killer to hurt anyone. Revan told him that he and his team would stand by him during the investigation. Perry thanked him and his team and left with Jones to the station.

Revan explained to the crime scene techs about what happened. He decided that there was nothing left for them to do. Everyone just wanted to go home so he called it a day. Revan's team got into their cars and left to head home for food and to write their reports.

Chapter 29

Holy crap that hurt. Who the heck shot me? It's not legal to shoot an unarmed man. These were the thoughts that screamed through his mind. He couldn't believe that he had been shot. The blood felt like it just kept coming out.

The medic in the ambulance with him kept telling him to lie still and not move. That was easy for him to say, he wasn't the one shot. If it wasn't for the guy in the grey windbreaker suit with the gun, he would have killed the medic. Windbreaker guy just sat there and looked at him with his gun in his hand. Pulse felt that the guy had his safety off and was just waiting for a reason.

The medic gave him a shot of something and the pain started going down a bit. With the receding of the pain, he was able to start laying still. With the pain leaving his mind, he was starting to think a little more clearly. He knew that he was in deep and needed a way out. He knew that they had all kinds of evidence against him. There was no legal way out of the mess. He needed something else. He needed an opportunity.

The ambulance hit a bump and the medic accidently jabbed his wound. The pain came back in a loud and clear message. It hit him so hard that he felt the world fading. He fought it as hard as he could. The pain kept up and he was running out of strength. The edges of his vision started to go black. No matter how hard he fought, the black took up more and more of his vision. As the darkness took up most of his vision, he gave one last push to stay awake. The darkness receded almost all the way. Then his strength felt like it was ripped away. The darkness flooded back in. The last moment before the darkness was complete, he felt the pulse begin.

He felt the world coming back. The world felt fuzzy and out of order. He felt like a fog had fallen on his mind. He tried to open his eyes and he couldn't get his eye lids to respond. After a moment of trying, he was about to give up. On his last try, they opened a little bit. A foggy bright light blinded him. He closed his eyes but decided to try to open his eyes again. As he opened his eyes, he heard a moan escape his lips. "Doctor, it looks like he's regaining consciousness," he heard a female nurse say. She sounded like she was far way. Her voice muffled by miles of space. A muffled beeping noise and millions of others jumbled together to blot out the background. He moved his head and eyes slightly. As he settled on a figure to his right, he saw a massive light green blob. The sight frightened him for a moment.

He saw the blob move and felt the massive pain again. The darkness rushed in faster that time. He wanted to fight it. He tried to gather up his fleeting strength. As he gathered it, he felt it rush away like water. He heard a louder muffled sound that was nearer but still far away. He felt the pulse again as the darkness took over.

He awoke again feeling the fog in his mind, his body and all round him. The world felt like a massive amount of fog. He pushed with all of his strength to open his eyes. A dull light hit his eyes. It was nowhere near as blinding as the last light. He stretched out his nerves trying to feel his body. As he reached farther and farther, he found a numb sensation in his arm and then the rest of his arm. His body tingled with the feeling. He felt his strength coming back. The fog was lifting from him. The world still held a slight fog but the rest was leaving him.

His sight managed to focus more as the fog left him. The fog faded from the world and he could pick out that he was in a room. Lights were on in the room but dimmed. He looked to his left and saw a metal pole next to his bed. He could see a plastic bag hanging from the pole and a tube flowing from it. As he followed the tube, he saw that it went into the top of his left hand. He could see a machine next to him that gave off a beeping sound with wires coming out of his shirt. He could see a green line that moved around and beeped when the line jumped up and down. He recognized it from TV on shows. He knew it kept track of his heart beat. He looked to his right to get his bearings.

The right wall had two big windows in it with blinds. The binds were closed. He could see shadows passing by it. A wood door was on the left wall past the windows near the far wall.

On the far wall were two more doors. He guessed that one was a closet and the other was a bathroom. He could see a wood chair in the corner of the far wall and the left wall. The left wall had a large window in the center of it with a blind that was closed. He looked up and could see a shelve above his head. He could not tell what was on the shelve from his position. The walls were painted white with a white drop down ceiling. He knew that he was in a standard oversized hospital bed with the plastic sides and all. He tried to move his head to see the floor and more of the room but found he could not move.

He gazed down at his body and saw something that made him wonder. His strength was returning more and more. He moved his feet first and felt them only move a little. The leather strap across his lower legs had two round straps in it. He knew this even though there was a blanket on his legs up to his waist. His feet were in those round straps and held tight. He felt a leather strap going across his midsection. He tried his arms next. His right arm was still numb in the upper arm. As he moved it, he felt pain again. He braced himself for the darkness to return but it didn't come. He moved his arms again and pressed pass the pain and tried moving. They would not move for him.

He laid back and cursed to himself. He knew that he had better stay quiet. He knew cops had to be outside of the room. If they knew he was awake, they would come in. He didn't want to deal with them or give them a reason to interrupt him. He knew that this would be his only chance to get out of there alive. He knew if he couldn't get one of his arms out, he was gonna have to deal with the cops.

He tried both of his arms again and felt the rest of the strap press against his back. He knew that his hurt arm would be too painful to mess around with too much. He twisted and moved his left arm forward and backward. As he moved his arm backward, he felt the back of his thumb on the strap. He pulled his arm back more and shifted his upper body to his right for more room. As he moved his arm, he tried folding his thumb into his palm. He could feel as his hand slowly pulled into the strap.

He stopped to relax his arm and hand. He felt his hand slide back out of the strap. He was discouraged by this but he knew he could get out. He rested a moment longer and began again. As he got his hand about half way in, he felt the IV catch on the strap. It hurt like heck but he kept pulling. He could feel the IV tearing out of his skin the more his hand moved. When his hand was most of the way in the strap, he rested for a moment.

He looked at the windows on his right and hoped that a nurse wouldn't come into the room or anyone want to check on him. After a second of rest, he started to pull again. He felt as the needle for the IV popped out of his hand. He pulled a little more and his hand came out of the strap. He wanted to get the rest of his straps right away but he was hurt and his left arm was tired.

He knew that someone would be there to check on him sometime soon and wanted to get the heck out. He resisted the urge to lay there and felt for the strap on his midsection. He found the buckle and the rest of the strap. It took some painful moving but he managed to get it unbuckled. Now that he could move most of his body, he twisted to his right a little. He got the buckle for that strap and undid it. He sat up in the bed to get his feet undone. He moved his right arm and shoulder by instinct. It hurt like heck but he wouldn't let it stop him. He pushed the blanket off of his feet and quickly undid those straps.

He swung his feet off of the bed to the left and got ready to stand up. He knew that it would be rough to stand but he never expected to nearly fall to the ground. He managed to catch himself but worried if he had made a noise. He braced himself for the cops to rush in but it never happened. He pushed himself and managed to stand up with a little wobble. He did all he could to keep quiet and not let a noise escape his lips.

Chapter 30

He looked at the heart monitor machine. He wanted it quiet and not to set off any alarms. He found a little knob on the front of the machine. He tested it and found that it did quiet the machine. He turned it down a little. As he did that, he heard voices outside the door. It sounded like a female talking to what sounded like two male voices. He knew that meant trouble but it could also be a good thing.

He managed to sit back on the bed. He swung his feet back on the bed. He pushed the straps to be under his feet to hold them down. He pulled the blanket over his legs. The strap for his midsection was lying down so he just laid on top of it. The blanket got pulled up over where the midsection strap should have gone over. He made the arm straps loose so he could take his arms out quickly. He put his hands in the straps and put his head on the pillow. His eyes closed just as the nurse entered the room.

As she closed the door, he realized that he had forgotten the IV for his hand. With that thought, another came into his mind. She could turn off the heart machine and help get him out of there.

She walked up to the heart machine and murmured to herself. She set her hand on the bed as she looked at the heart monitor. While she was preoccupied, he slid his left hand out of the strap. He opened his eyes just enough to see where she was. She was close to the bed. She had a clip board in her hand but it would do her no good. The pulse rose quickly and he reached with his hand just as quickly.

He grabbed her neck with all of his strength. He squeezed hard so she would not make a sound. He remembered his human biology classes well and squeezed where he knew the voice box was. He pressed hard with his thumb and forefinger. She didn't make a sound outside of a faint whisper. She dropped the clip board on his bed by instinct and his luck.

He looked at her young face, with her shoulder length hair falling into her face. Her brown eyes welled up with tears and fear. Her thin body trembled under her flower nurse scrubs. He watched a moment as her large breast shook and made him long for a feel. The pulse snapped him back to the issue at hand.

He pulled her close to him and said quietly, "I want you to turn that heart machine off. It had better not make a sound or send anybody running in here." Tears started to fall down her cheeks. One tear hit the corner of her mouth and slid across her full lips. "If someone comes in here, I will still have time to kill you. I will rape you as I kill you and see that your body is displayed all over the news. Do you understand me?"

She nodded her head yes with more tears coming. He swung his legs off the bed again. That time they were stronger and didn't fail him. He maneuvered so she could face the heart monitor. She touched the face of the machine and pressed an orange button. It had a bell symbol with a slash through it above the button.

He reached in his shirt with his right hand. It hurt like heck but he didn't let it show. He pulled off the wires that connected him to the machine. He pulled her over to the window. He slowly pulled up the blind and looked outside. He could see that he was on the second floor. It would hurt like heck but he knew he had his chance. It was dark outside so he knew that he had been out for a while.

He said to her, “Open the window and push out the screen.” She looked at him puzzled but did as she was told. She pushed the screen out after a few pushes. “Sit up on the window sill. Remember, don’t do anything stupid.” She did as she was told. He leaned close to her again and said, “Just remember this, I never said I would let you live. I just don’t feel like raping you or have enough time to do my full work.”

She looked with complete terror at him and began to fight as he squeezed. He already had a good grip on her neck and was holding her tightly. He squeezed tighter and felt her airway crush. A moment later she went completely limp. He knew that he was running out of time in the room. He held her too long already.

He grabbed her body against his. His right arm throbbed. He turned holding her and sat on the window sill. He pushed himself out of the window. He twisted as he left the window and put her body below his. They landed on a bush next to the building. With the bush and her body, it helped break his fall. As he stood up, there was a solid white wall next to him. It made him glad so no one would see him.

He looked at himself quickly and saw what he was wearing. He was wearing a pair of blue hospital pants and a blue shirt that was open to reveal his chest. The right sleeve of his shirt was cut off and he had no shoes on. A big white bandage was wrapped around his upper right arm. A little bit of blood was starting to show on the inside of the bandage. He knew that the fall must have opened up the wound again. It would have to be taken care of but not right away. It was time to leave and stay gone.

He walked out to the parking lot. He made sure that he held his shirt closed. He didn't want anyone to stop. He saw that a guy was getting out of his car. He quietly jogged up to the car. It was a white sedan, he wasn't sure what kind.

As he was near he said, "Hey, give me your keys man." The guy looked at him in surprised. He had his keys in his hand when Pulse grabbed him. Pulse grabbed him by the back of the hair. He slammed the guy's face into the top edge of the car. The guy fell down dazed. Pulse grabbed him again and slammed his head into the side of the car. He went down like a sack of bricks.

Pulse grabbed the keys and got in the car. He slammed the door shut and started the car. Pulse thanked god that the guy only had three keys on ring. He backed out of the spot. He wanted to run the guy over but knew that it would damage the car and draw attention. He got on the road and hit the freeway.

He didn't have a specific place that he wanted to go to. He just wanted to leave the city behind. He knew that the only way to disappear was to have money. He didn't have his wallet or anything else to get to his money. He saw the signs on the freeway and made a decision.

He followed the sign that said Detroit. He hit the gas as he got out of the city limits. He wanted to get to Detroit as soon as he could. There he could get rid of the car and find a place to hide. It would give him a chance to do some work and get some money from that person. He could then get a new car and disappear.

As he drove, he didn't think about his speed or where he was. All of a sudden, he saw a red flashing light in his rear view mirror. He pulled over to the side of the road. He had no idea if he was gone long enough for the car to be reported stolen. He also knew that no matter what, this was not a good thing. He could not prove the car was his or why he was going so fast.

The pulse started in his mind. He knew what he had to do. He turned off the car and took out the keys. He put each key in between each finger of his right hand. He sat there looking in his rear view mirror. The cop just sat there in his car talking on the radio. Pulse felt like he was taking forever. He knew he was gonna have to take matters into own hands.

He got out of the car after a car passed. He walked to the cop car. The cop looked up when he was almost the whole way there. The pulse kept pounding. He needed to do this. One more kill to help him disappear.

The cop got out of his car with his hand on his gun. He looked like a young guy, just a rookie state cop. Pulse kept slowly walking to the door. The cop commanded, “Get back in your car sir. I will be with you in a moment.” Pulse continued forward. “Stay back sir or I will be forced to taze you.” Pulse was at the door. “Back off sir or you will be tazed.”

As the officer started to pull on his taser, Pulse swung his right hand with all of his strength. The officer fell to the ground. Pulse was on top of him in a split second. He drove the keys deep into the cop’s throat. He punch him a few more times to make sure that he was dead. No cars were on the road. He knew he would not have long till one did.

He picked the cop up and dragged him to the white car. He put him in the front seat. He ripped off the shirt of the cop uniform and the weapons belt.

He went back to the officer’s car and put on the shirt and belt. He found the officer’s hat and found the switch for the lights. He turned off the radio and pulled away. He knew that the disguise would help him hide till he got to Detroit. He kept his speed down so he would blend in.

Chapter 31

Revan and his team stopped in Durand just outside of Flint. They all were hungry and a bit excited from the bust. They found a small family restaurant just off the freeway on Lansing road. On the way there, Revan was informed by Flint police that the killer was taken to McLaren hospital. He was told that Dranns had passed out on the way to the hospital. The wound looked like it was a clean through and through but they would be 100% sure after the doctor looked at him. They told him that Dranns would probably be kept overnight for observation but kept under guard.

It was a small place with a rustic look. Booths lined the walls looking out the windows. The booths had a teal leather cover. A table counter looked into the kitchen. The stools had the same teal leather as the booths. Old metal tables and chairs filled in the rest of the room. The room was decorated in paintings that depict rural scenes. Old wooden planks filled in the walls without windows. Fading white and teal tiles covered the floor.

After they all sat down, a waitress came

up wearing a pink uniform from the 50s. She took their orders and left them to talk. "Ok, ok, ok. I gotta ask you this question Revan," John said gesturing to Revan's leather jacket. "Why the heck do you have two guns in a shoulder holster? It's not like this is an action movie. Shooting like that doesn't work." The others looked to Revan for an answer.

"No, shooting like an idiot with two guns never works out. But if you are a good shot with one hand, then you can work to two. If a person is ambidextrous then they can learn easier. I'm not one but I worked hard and taught myself. I had to learn because I broke my right arm once and needed to know how to shoot with my left. It took me quite a while but I did it. After my arm healed, I kept practicing with both and started to use two," Revan said sitting back in his chair.

Those kind of talks continued for a while. They all got their food quickly. Darkness began to fall as they ate and talked about the day. After they ate Revan got a call. "Is this Lieutenant Revan Lygar," a voice asked.

Revan got a bad feeling answering the phone. “Yes this is. Who is this and how can I help you,” Revan asked. The others a looked at him and he could tell they had the same feeling as him.

The voice said, “This is Officer Bond of the Flint police department. We need to you to come to McLaren hospital right away. The prisoner Theodore Dranns has escaped and killed a nurse. He beat up a guy and stole his car. He is on the run.”

Revan nearly yelled, “Jesus Christ!” He looked at his team and said, “Everybody get in the cars, Dranns has escaped. We gotta get to McLaren hospital right now.” Revan held the phone between his shoulder and ear as he stood up. He pulled out his wallet and threw a $100 on the table. The others got up and walked with Revan to the door. Revan said to the phone, “We’ll be there in a few minutes. Update me if you get anything new.” He hung up the phone before the officer could answer him.

They all got in the two cars and pulled out. The cars pulled on to the freeway and headed for Flint at top speed. John Barry and

Amy rode with Revan and the others rode with Mary. As they neared Flint, Revan got a call from the officer again.

"Lieutenant Lygar, this is Officer Bond again, we have an update for you," he said. "We got a call from the state police. He is in a state police patrol car heading in the direction of Detroit."

Revan grunted a reply and tossed the phone to Barry. He told him to talk to the officer and get the information they needed. Barry talked to the officer while Revan drove stepping on the gas more. He could see Mary in his rear view mirror keeping up with him. He found the exit for Detroit and got on I-75. He hit the gas harder with Mary on his heels.

Barry talked for a bit and then put down the phone. He said, "They did something really stupid that will bite them in the rear." Revan looked at him with a raised eyebrow. "When the doc was patching up Dranns, he regained consciousness for a moment. Just as the doc was gonna say something to him, he went out again. They put him in a private room on the second floor. The Flint police put two officers on his room. Because Dranns was still out and the docs felt that he was gonna be out for a long while; the officers stayed outside the room. While he was out, they put him in leather restraints. A nurse, Becky Lynn 24, came by to get readings for paperwork. Because Dranns was still out and tied up, the officers let her in the room alone. Everyone winced at the stupidity of the decision.

"Sometime between when he was put in the room and the nurse showed up, Dranns got loose. They aren't sure yet by they think he woke up and somehow got a hand out of a restraint. He undid the rest and got the nurse when she came in. He made her turn off the heart monitor they had him hooked up to. They hooked him up to it just in case there was an issue with the wound they were unaware of. He strangled her and opened the window in his room." Revan looked at Barry in a way that said 'are they really that stupid'.

Barry shrugged and said, "He used her body to help break his fall to the ground. He got up and went into the parking lot. He found a guy getting out of his car and beat the snot out of him and took the car. While he was getting the car, the officers checked the room wondering why the nurse didn't come out. When they saw the open window, they saw the nurse laying on the ground outside of it and Dranns tearing butt out of the lot. That's when they got a hold of us. While we were heading to the hospital, Dranns got pulled over between exits 108 and 109."

"Jesus this is bad," Amy said from the back. "Those fools could not have screwed up any more if they had untied him themselves."

"A rookie state trooper pulled him over for speeding," Barry continued. "Just as he managed to radio in that he pulled over the car Dranns stole, Dranns came up to him. Dranns killed him with what looked like car keys. He took the officers shirt and belt, he got in the patrol car and continued on his way. We did get a break out of this one though. Because the trooper was just a rookie, he got the car with the GPS tracker. They activated the GPS after the trooper failed to report in before he was found a moment later. They have been calling orders to avoid Dranns getting wind. The state guys are handling their guy and we are free to catch up. They said that it looks like he is driving the speed limit to avoid being looked at too hard."

Revan kept the gas on and had Barry relay the info to Mary's car. He didn't want Dranns anywhere near Detroit. He knew that it would be hard if Dranns found out that they were nearing him. What worried Revan the most was that Dranns had the rookie's sidearm and the shotgun in the car. He knew that if they caught up to Dranns and didn't get the drop on him, it would lead to a shoot out. His only hope was that maybe Dranns wouldn't be able to release the shotgun from the car.

Barry got on his phone and got a hold of the state police tracking the stolen patrol car. They kept him updated on the speed and the location of the car. As Revan neared Springfield, he was told that Dranns made Independence Charter Township. He worried because he was also told that Dranns had picked up speed. Revan knew that it was bad because Dranns had the patrol car with the pursuit engine and he would have to rely on his aftermarket one in the BMW.

As he put on a steady amount of speed, he got told that Dranns was making distance on him. He knew that his car and Mary's wouldn't be able to hold up the pursuit for much longer.

Dranns slowed down nearing Auburn Hills and Revan hoped to catch him. He got in sight of the patrol car and crept up closer. As he got within 50 yards of the car, Dranns stepped on the gas. He knew that this chase was really on.

Chapter 32

The chase continued on nearing the exit for Pontiac. Dranns kept on his speed and so did Revan. Dranns had pushed his cruiser harder when he neared exit 79. Revan moved in and kept him away from the exit but knew he couldn't do it forever. Dranns tried for exit 78 but Mary got up and kept him from it. Revan didn't want him to get on a city street with innocent people. The killer went for 77B but that time they couldn't get up in time to stop him. With the exit down to one lane, Revan couldn't get beside him. He saw that Dranns was pushing the patrol car too hard and was barely keeping it on the road. He knew that if the chase kept up much longer that it was going to end badly.

As Dranns merged onto 59, he just barely beat out a semi truck. Revan and Mary got slowed by the semi. They slammed on the gas to get around the truck and catch up to Dranns again. As Revan closed the distance, he saw Dranns take exit 39. Dranns nearly lost control around the turn but regained it hitting north Opdyke road. Dranns headed south as

Revan and Mary got on the exit. Dranns sped up faster trying to out distance himself. Revan caught up to Dranns and tried to cut him off. Dranns took a hard right turn onto Auburn Avenue. He couldn't keep the patrol car under control and managed to put it into the parking lot of what looked like an abandoned building without losing complete control.

The building was large and looked to have been a warehouse or shipping center. The white paint was fading and there were stains from when a company name was once there. Two out of the five windows in the front of the building were broken. The rest of the windows were filthy. The door was dented and left hanging open. The parking lot lights were out but the full moon shined bright on the parking lot. The parking lot had deeply faded parking space lines. Trash was littered throughout the lot.

Dranns decided to abandon the stolen car as Revan and Mary pulled into the lot. Amy pointed out that it looked like the killer was messing with something before he got out running. Dranns ran to the building and slammed through the door. He kicked the door shut and disappeared into the darkness. The whole team got out of the cars with guns in their hands. They moved up slowly with their guns pointed at the windows and the door. They wanted to be ready if Dranns started shooting. Ray moved to the abandoned patrol car to see if he could see what Dranns was doing.

He motioned for Revan to come near. He told him that Dranns was probably trying to get the shotgun but couldn't get the holder to disengage. Revan nodded that he believed so too. Revan had Ray call in back up. He motioned his team to move up to the building. As they lined the wall, he looked to Barry, Amy, Ray and John. He told them to split up and move around the building. John and Ray went around the right side and Barry and Amy went to the left.

Revan and his small team entered the building. The darkness was blinding. Revan and Mary had flashlights from their vehicles. They were standing in what looked like a former greeting room. A counter was against the wall for a secretary. To the left was a hall with doors.

On the wall by the hallway was a sign that said offices with an arrow pointing to the hallway. To the right was a set of doors with a sign that said shipping. Revan motioned for Mary and Eric to sweep the offices. Derek and he moved to a set of double doors.

As they entered the shipping room, they could see that it was a very large room. To their right was a stair well that headed up the wall to a long hallway. In the hallway were more offices. The shipping room had old conveyer belts and even some abandoned crates. A tipped over fork lift laid in the center of the room next to a tipped pile of packages. Various other pieces of shipping equipment were left in the room turning it into a maze.

Revan handed Derek the flashlight and told him to head up and check the offices. Derek told him that they both should go. Revan said, “No, you get up there and check. I don’t want us both to go somewhere and let this guy get by us. If you have to, shoot him dead. I don’t care. He needs to be put down. Now take the light and head up there.” Revan motioned for Derek to head up the stairs. Derek kept the light off as he headed up the stairs silently and flipped it on when he made it in the walled hallway.

Revan turned on his other light, the one that he had in his right gun. After giving Derek the light, he pulled out his left gun. He moved slowly through the maze of items keeping low. The light cast shadows all over the room. He knew that the light would give him away but he didn't want to be running around blind. He heard a noise near the left side of the room farther in. It sounded like someone had ran into something. Revan put his light low as he made his way through the maze. He kept his left gun up in case he needed to shoot.

As he moved around objects, the room seemed so much larger than it should be. For an abandoned shipping building, he couldn't believe that they had left so much stuff behind. He settled by one of the conveyer belts to take a look around. He raised his head to look around. A shadow moved about 50 feet away and made a thudding noise.

He wanted to call out or take a shot but knew he had better not. The shadow and noise could be an animal or even a homeless person hiding out in there. He still kept his light low and moved to get closer. He had to move the long way around to avoid climbing. It would have made more noise than he was willing to risk and also made him an easy target.

He wound his way through the maze. As he moved, he kept hearing more noises. When he got within 20 feet of the noises, he turned off his light. The darkness made his speed next to nothing. He was willing to go as slow as he needed to keep from making any sound. He put his left gun in its holster and used the hand to help guide his way. The hand led the way while he kept listening for noises.

As his ears adjusted to listen for more sounds. His ears brought him sounds from where Derek was. He could hear Derek wondering in the upstairs offices. The occasional banging from a door opening came from that direction. He heard a rat skitter by him. A bird or a bat flapped over head. The sound of wind came from the right side of the building near the back. The only guess Revan had was that a door or a loading dock door was left a little open. The dusty decaying smell was all around him. The smell of sweat came from somewhere to his front and left. The sound of heavy breathing came from the same direction.

His adrenalin kicked in as his heart beat faster. He moved in the direction of the sound and smell. He closed in and felt that he was within 10 to 15 feet of the killer. He slowly reached in and upholstered his left gun. He felt slowly in front of him. He found what he was looking for, a crate of boxes between him and the killer. The crate was short so he could stand up and see over it but he could hide behind it. He stood slowly and could feel his knees wanting to crack from being bent for too long. He just hoped he would be able to train his guns on the killer before the cracks would come.

He was too late, his knees cracked just as he was turning on his light. A shot rang out and a bullet buried into another crate of items next to him. He went down quickly but got off a few shots as he went into hiding. The shots echoed throughout the room. He heard the killer running away from him and smack into something. A curse erupted from the killer.

Revan stood again and pointed his guns in the directions. His light only showed objects in his way. He moved forward and caught a glimpse of the killer. He yelled, "Dranns, freeze or I will shoot. Put your hands up!"

Another shot was fired in Revan's direction. Revan fired back but knew that he wouldn't get him. As he made his way forward, he heard a noise coming from behind him. He heard Mary and Eric come through the double doors. Derek made his way down the stairs and join up with Mary and Eric. They started shouting to Revan wondering if he was hit. Revan slowed and called out to them so they would know that he was alright.

His main concern was that the killer was loose in there and that he may find his way out. The only hope that he had was that the others outside heard the shots and would catch Dranns if he got out.

He made his way to the back of the building through the maze to get to the only area of escape. When he neared, he heard some shouting from outside and one single shot. He put on more speed feeling dread.

Chapter 33

It took him a minute to make his way to the opening; it was a door that led out to loading docks. A handful of shots rang out as he neared the door. When he made his way outside, he saw Ray kneeling on the ground next to a dark shape. Ray motioned Revan over in a frantic gesture. He could hear stumbling and shouting coming from inside the building behind him. The dread that Revan felt deepened as he neared Ray.

He was kneeling next to a body. In the moon light, he could see the person was wearing a suit, the same kind worn by FBI agents. There was only one agent in the area he knew about. It was John laying there on the ground. Blood was coming from a wound in his left shoulder. A lot of blood was seeping onto the ground. Ray had taken off his long sleeve t-shirt. He was using it on the wound to stop the bleeding. Ray told him that after he heard the shot, he came running. When he got there, he saw a dark shape running into the woods and John on the ground. He was the one that fired the other shots. Ray hoped that he could at least injure Dranns. At that time it seemed like everyone showed up at once. Mary, Derek and Eric came out of the warehouse and Barry and Amy came running around from the back of the building.

Revan told them to search the woods for the killer and if they need to, shoot to kill. Revan didn't like the FBI but he wasn't about ready for one to die on his watch. As they headed into the woods by the warehouse, a state police car showed up. He gripped John's hand quickly and ran to the patrol car.

The patrol car stopped and the officer stepped out and asked what was going on. Revan said quickly, "I am Lieutenant Revan Lygar of the Michigan Serial Killer Investigation Unit. We were here trying to apprehend a killer. He shot one of my agents. We need an ambulance right away. Then get your first aid kit and do what you can for my guy." Revan started to jog away. He said over his shoulder, "Put out an alert for Theodore Dranns. He is a violent serial killer and armed with a gun that he took from a cop that he killed. He will kill without hesitation."

Revan and his team scoured the woods

looking for any sign of the killer. In the darkness they couldn't find anything. After about 10 minutes of searching, more officers showed up and helped with the combing of the woods. One of the officers informed Revan that John was in an ambulance and being taken to a local hospital.

The search continued for another two hours in the sweltering heat. Everyone was sweating and getting tired. Revan had his team leave the woods to regroup. As they left the woods, Revan had to deal with the local police chief. He explained to the chief the whole situation. The more he talked, the more the chief's face grew grave.

After the talk, the chief called in to get more officers out into the area. An officer got out a map and placed it on the hood of his car. Revan looked at the map as the chief spoke commands into the radio. He sent officers to various areas in force hoping that he was getting them there before the killer could get by. Revan knew that they knew the area better than him and his team so he just stood back.

The chief turned to Revan after he got

off the radio and said, “Well Lieutenant Lygar, this search could take some time to complete. If you would like, you can stay here and wait for news or you can head home and we’ll get a hold of you if we find anything. If you would like we can find a place nearby to stay.”

Revan replied, “It’s ok, we’ll head out of here and get home. You guys know the area and it could take some time till anything is found. That is if he can even be found now.” He shook hands with the chief. “We’ll move out of here and please don’t forget to send over any evidence to our labs. Thanks for the assistance. Please let me know if you hear anything on my agent between now and morning. I’m gonna come back then to see how he’s doing.”

Revan and his team got into their cars to leave. As they pulled away from the scene, a media van was just going by. Revan felt relief that they must have got held up before getting to the warehouse. They headed back to the freeway wanting to just backtrack to Flint and then to Muskegon. They got onto 59 heading west so they could get on 75 north.

A short time after getting on 59, Revan saw a car on the side of the road with its hazard lights on. A man was standing by the car with his arms waving in the air trying to flag them down. Barry suggested that they stop. Revan agreed and pulled over. Mary pulled over behind him and asked what was going on. He told her that a guy needed help so he was stopping.

He walked up to the man by the stopped car. Revan asked him, “What’s going on sir? What can I help you with?”

“Do you have a phone? I need you to call police immediately,” the man said very frantic. “There was a hit and run. I think the guy is dead. He looks like he could be a cop or something.”

Revan started walking forward and said, “I’m a cop. Please head back to my car and tell my team what happened and to call for a unit immediately. I’ll see about the guy that was hit. After the call, tell them to come up here right away.” The man ran back to Revan’s car while he continued to walk forward.

The words “looks like a cop” rang in his

head. He didn't think that it could be true. He reached the front of the car and entered into the head lights. In the lights on the side of the road was a vaguely human form. It looked like it was covered in a sports coat. He can only think that it must be the driver's coat.

He neared the body and kneeled on the road. He saw that the body had blue hospital pants and no shoes on. The feet were dirty and had a few cuts on the soles. He pulled the coat slowly back and saw the top of a state trooper uniform. He looked at the face and medium length hair. He knew who it was right away. Revan felt for a pulse and came up empty. The rest of his team walked up behind him. They asked what was going on. He told them to look at the face. They all just stared in disbelief.

As they all just looked at the body, a patrol car showed up. The officer walked up and asked Revan what was going on. He replied, "You guys can call off your search for the killer." The officer asked why. "Because someone found the killer for us. It was a hit and run, I guess we can just close the file on him. I'll let you guys handle this mess. Send me a copy of the death certificate.” The officer said ok and took their statements. He then let them all leave. Revan and his team went home unsatisfied with the closing of the case.

Chapter 34

A week and a half later, John was transferred from Havenwyck Hospital in Auburn Hills to Mercy Hospital in Muskegon. He was still recovering from his gun shot. The team went out to see him while he was still in Auburn Hills. His health condition was shaky for the first few days from blood loss. On the first night he flat lined and was almost declared dead. By the fourth day in the hospital, he was in good condition. When the doctors were satisfied with his health, they allowed the transfer. Revan only saw him once while he was in Auburn Hills. That was the first day and John was still out to the world.

The amount of paperwork buried the whole team for at least two days. Revan was barraged by the feds and by the press. It took many of Revan's resources to keep the press away from John's room in the hospital. The chief held a press conference the day after Dranns died. She laid out the standard story to the hollys and answered a number of questions. Revan was present at that conference. He got up and told the end of the case involving the hit and run and John's shooting. He gave John's condition and stepped away from the podium. As he moved away, the hollys attacked him with questions that he did not answer. The chief tried to berate him after the conference for not answering the hollys questions but gave up when she could see that he really didn't care.

On John's first day in Mercy, Revan went up to see him. He made his way to John's room after talking to the doctor. The doctor informed Revan that John would be released the next day but would have to take it easy at work till he recovered. Revan knew that a lot of physical therapy was in John's immediate future.

He went into John's room and saw him laying on the bed watching the TV. When he saw Revan enter the room, he turned off the TV and adjusted his sling. As he moved his sling, John winced in obvious pain. He said, "Hey Lieutenant. How are you doing? Why haven't I seen you? The others came by to see me. Well I guessed that you just didn't care about me because I'm an FBI agent."

"I did come by to see you. It was just the

first day," Revan said sitting down in a chair next to John's bed. "After the first day, I spent time having to finish up the case and get it closed. I also had to deal with those media idiots. I still get them from time to time but it's less than before. Did the others tell you about Dranns?" John nodded yes. "Yeah, it's a crappy way to close a case but at least it's over. The media tried giving us crap over it but the chief shut them up. She knew I wasn't going to do it alone. Did you have a visit from your bosses?"

"Yeah I did. They grilled me about the case till they were sure I didn't have any more to tell them. I was told that they talked to you before they came to see me. They didn't like how you ran things but I don't think they knew how to deal with it. They warned me that if I screwed up or didn't get things done their way, I would be fired. By the way, why didn't we have an arrest warrant for Dranns? They didn't ask me about it but I wondered," John inquired.

"Well, I won't be surprised if they try and screw me over sometime so they can shut us down. On the warrant side, we didn't need one. Our group has a special condition from my former bosses so one is not needed for us. Your bosses already knew and hate it. The reason is that with serial killers, we are in a time sensitive situation. If we know who the suspect is, then we gotta get them before they can kill again. By the way, I got something I want to show you first before everyone else," replied Revan.

"Oh ok. I can see the sense in not needing an arrest warrant for a serial killer. They tend to kill people in shortening time frames," John said back. "So what is it you want to show me? And why do you want me to see first?"

Revan stood up and placed a piece of paper and a post card on John. He said, "I like you. You have proven that you are a good guy and a member of my team. You have a position with us even if the feds let you go. All you gotta do is keep learning to follow your instincts. That and you have a crap load of paperwork to fill out when you get out of here. I had a thought of sending it up here for you to work on but didn't want to get the whining from your docs about hurting you more."

Revan gestured to the objects on John's

lap. “This is a card I got in the mail. It’s from the mystery caller. The one that told us about the cold case up state.” John nodded yes that he remembered. “It thanks us for getting the killer and hopes that we will clear other crimes he committed. The other is the death certificate for Theodore Dranns.” John gave him a questioning look. “Take a look at the signature of Dranns’ mother on the certificate and the writing on the card.”

John looked closely at both pieces of writing. He began looking harder and faster going back and forth. After a minute of studying them both, he looked up at Revan with a look of dumbfounded surprise.

CPSIA information can be obtained
at www.ICGtesting.com
Printed in the USA
LVOW04s0055221016
509645LV00011B/135/P